Irish Crossings
Michael's Story

IRISH CROSSINGS

MICHAEL'S STORY

TERENCE O'LEARY

ALSO BY
TERENCE O'LEARY

Swan
Creek
Press

First Swan Creek Press, LLC Edition 2020
ISBN: 9781733534123

www.terenceoleary.com

Design: Heather McIntyre, Cover&Layout |
www.coverandlayout.com
Cover Photo © Alessandro Cancian
Author's photo by Shena Kaye

For my Sisters
Peggy, Patty, Pam,
Colleen & Nancy

In Memory of
Patrick and Catherine Feeney

They led their children out of Ireland during the time of the Great Hunger. They didn't survive the voyage to America, but their son, my grandfather's grandfather, lived to tell their story.

"It is in the shelter of each other that people live."

– An ancient Irish proverb

Irish Crossings
Michael's Story

Caitlin worried her lower lip so hard that it almost bled. White knuckles gripped the steering wheel. She quickly veered into the parking spot. The front tire bounced off the curb. She snapped off the ignition, snatched the keys, and was out of the car before the engine died.

Icy air raced across the open field. The teenager lifted her coat collar and ducked her head into its shelter. She raced to the front door of the Emily Scott Nursing Home. She didn't stop at the front desk, but ran down the brightly lit hallway. The door to Gigi's room was shut. She stopped, drew a deep breath, and opened the door.

A nurse hovered over her beloved great-grandmother. The nurse was dressed in white and Caitlin thought she looked like an angel. Caitlin took small, quiet steps to the bed.

The nurse said, "I'm so sorry."

"I came as fast as I could," the words tumbled out all in one breath.

"I came to check on Irma this morning. I thought she was just sleeping."

Caitlin reached and gently caressed Gigi's cold hand.

"She just never woke up," the nurse said.

Caitlin didn't feel the tears rolling down her cheeks. "I just wanted to be here when it was time so that she wouldn't be alone."

"She didn't suffer. She just passed away in her sleep. Maybe she was dreaming."

Caitlin leaned forward and kissed Gigi's forehead. The teenager's long red, curly hair fell upon Gigi's white pillow.

"Ninety-eight," the nurse said. "That's a long life."

"She had a full and happy life." Caitlin smiled through her tears and lovingly stroked Gigi's cheek. "I'm so going to miss her and her stories. No one could tell a story like my Gigi." She sighed. "Now her stories are gone with her."

The nurse moved to the night table. "A package came for her yesterday. Irma was all excited." The nurse lifted a large brown envelope. "She had me read her the letter that came with the package. The letter's from one of your distant cousins." She slid a heavy black covered book from the envelope. "Your cousin, William, said he found the book in an old wooden box in their attic. He said they're moving and he stumbled across the book. He thought Irma should have it."

She handed the book to Caitlin.

The book was old. The edges were worn. A smoky, musty smell arose as Caitlin opened the cover. Some of pages had yellowed and a few were water stained. The small, cursive handwriting was hard for Caitlin to read.

"Your cousin said the book seemed to be a journal."

Caitlin gave a quick inquisitive look from the journal to her great-grandmother.

"Irma said that she saw the book once before. She said it was a long, long time ago when she visited Garryowen. She was so excited for you to read the book to her. She said it was Michael's Story."

Caitlin's face brightened. "Three brothers came from Ireland during the time of the Great Hunger. Michael was the youngest." Caitlin looked to the nurse. "Can I sit with Gigi for a while?"

The nurse nodded. "I need to make some calls. I'll be back later."

The nurse left and Caitlin pulled a chair to the bedside. She rested the book on the white comforter next to her great-grandmother. She opened the cover and read Michael's Story to her Gigi.

IRELAND 1847
THE GREAT HUNGER

Chapter 1

My life was a gift from my brother. If it wasn't for Danny, I would have died in Ireland like so many others.

The potatoes were our food and when the potatoes turned black there was nothing left to eat. Every day, I would go with my ma and my sisters out to the fields. We'd scrounge for anything. Turnips and carrots were treasured. Whatever we found, we would take home and Ma would make soup. We would not eat until my da and Danny came back to the cottage. They'd leave before the sun rose and come home after it set. They would work all day breaking and carrying stones to build a road that Da said went nowhere. If we were lucky, Da would bring home a bag of rice. Ma would add the rice to the soup.

Ma would make us pray before she'd let our wooden spoons scoop our soup. Da would not pray. He'd sit still at the table with his spoon clenched in his fist. I'll never forget the look on his face as he stared at his soup. He was a hard man. The famine just made him harder. While we ate, our house was as solemn as our church.

I slept with my brother. Danny was 10. He was two years older than me. The work on the road was hard for a man and much more bone wearying for a boy. I remember the first time Danny came home after carrying rocks all day. He fell asleep at the table before he even finished his soup. My da shook him awake. He fed Danny like a child. He wouldn't let Danny sleep until the soup was gone.

At night in our bed, I would wait until Danny would start softly snoring, I would snuggle next to him. I was always cold and the fire was far from our bed.

It would take me a long time to fall asleep. My mind would wander. I would try to think of happy times, but they were getting harder and harder to remember. At one time we had a cow and a pig. My oldest brother, Paddy, would watch over them so that no one would steal what was ours, but it didn't matter. Coghlan, Lord Townsend's agent, took our cow when Da couldn't pay the rent. We had no food to feed our pig so the pig fed us.

When Da would go to bed, my ma and my sisters would kneel by the fire and pray their rosary. Da would turn his back to them and cover his head with his arm.

Sometimes, when the wind blew at night, I thought I could hear Uncle Seamus's fiddle. It brought back the last happy time that I could remember: Paddy and Caitlin's wedding. We had a party at our cottage. We still had food back then, but not much. The neighbors brought what little they had to share. Uncle Seamus played his fiddle and it was like he took away all of our cares. He took us to another time. Caitlin and Paddy danced. She was so beautiful. She was 16, the same age as Paddy. At 16, Paddy was already a man. He was taller than my da, but he was not a hard man. Paddy left before the famine could make him hard.

Danny sang at the wedding feast. Ma always said that Danny had the voice of an angel. When Danny sang, my da's face changed. I saw a man I never knew, a quiet, thoughtful man who hid inside his gruff exterior.

Caitlin and Paddy danced in the field in the shadows of my ancestors. Da said at one time our family owned all our land, but the English came and took it from us. Now, we pay rent to Lord Townsend to farm the land that once was ours.

Caitlin and Paddy left the day after the wedding. They went to America. They went to stay with Uncle Richard, my da's brother. Uncle Richard is a blacksmith in Philadelphia. Paddy will work with him and learn how to be a blacksmith. Paddy said he would send money back to Ireland so that we could all go to America, but Paddy left a long time ago and we are still here.

CHAPTER 2

Winter came and the British said there was no more money to pay for the roads. They turned their back on us. Da would still get up early in the morning and go to town. He'd search for any work that was there to be had. Some days he would bring home some food, but most days he came home with nothing. He'd sit in his chair and stare at the fire. We all knew not to bother him.

We'd scrounge the fields farther and farther from home. Our pickings were slim and at night our soup was mostly water.

Danny wouldn't come with us to the fields. He'd go off by himself, but he was always home before dark. Danny was scared of the dark. Unlike my da, Danny always seemed to bring something home with him. One day, he brought home a dead rabbit. I remember Ma made the sign of the cross over the rabbit and cried. That night we all had a small piece of Danny's gift. I had forgotten what meat tasted like.

Danny started bringing home other things: one day a shovel, another day a pot. Whatever he brought home, he would give to Da, who would take it to town. Da would sell or pawn what Danny gave him. If we were lucky, Da would have enough money to bring home some rice.

I have two sisters, Mary, who is 15, and Joanna, who is 14. Mary was always quick with her tongue. One night after we finished dinner, Mary asked Danny if he was stealing. Da's hand moved so fast it was a blur. He slapped Mary's cheek. My sister reeled and quickly stood. She ran to her bed.

Danny said loud enough for Mary to hear, "I don't steal." He looked to our ma. "Some of our neighbors are gone. I just take what they've left behind. That's not stealing."

"Where did they go?" Joanna asked in a timid voice.

Danny glanced at Joanna and then turned so that he could face Mary as she sat on the side of her bed. "Where did they go? If you really want to know, go down to the Hegartys'. They're there but they're not there. They're all in one bed and they're all dead. They just gave up and stopped trying." Danny looked to our father. "We do what we must to survive."

Our da had taught Danny well.

CHAPTER 3

Some days if the rain was too cold to scrounge the fields, my sisters would beg Ma to let them go down to Brigid's cabin. They'd whine and plead until Ma would finally give her blessing. Ma always made my sisters take me with them. I didn't want to leave Ma alone, but I so wanted to go to Brigid's. Ma would button my coat. She'd put one of Danny's old caps, that he outgrew, on my curly brown hair. She'd kiss my cheeks and hug me tight against her chest.

Brigid was Caitlin's younger sister. We could see her cabin from our doorway. At one time, I could run through the rain to her cottage, but I no longer had the energy to run. I'd trudge the path with my head down and my hands in my pockets. Rain would soak the back of my shirt beneath my collar.

Brigid was only 7 and she was small like me. There were two brothers born between her and Caitlin. Her father had sent the boys to stay with his brother in Cork. Brigid's da, like mine, would go to town to search for work. I don't know if he had more luck or if it was because they had fewer people to feed, but they always seemed to have some food in their cottage. I'd hang my coat by the fire and wait as patiently as I could as Brigid's ma made us porridge.

Now that Caitlin and Paddy were married, we were family. Brigid's ma asked us to call her Aunt Sarah. The porridge was warm and tickled my stomach. It was only made with water, not milk and butter, but it still was so good.

The girls would go off to play. They wouldn't include me because I was a boy, but I didn't mind. I'd much rather spend time with Aunt Sarah. She knew how to read and write. No one in my family could even write their name. Aunt Sarah and I would sit at the table by the fire with pencils and paper. I never knew that letters could make words and words could tell a story. I asked her how she learned to read. She told me as a child she was an orphan. She was raised by the good sisters. The nuns taught her how to read and write.

Aunt Sarah said I had a gift. None of her children could pick up the letters as quick as I did. The first time I wrote my name, I swelled with pride. Aunt Sarah ruffled my hair and smiled.

Rain beat on the thatch above our heads. The cottage was warm and smoky. Aunt Sarah gave me the keys to a world I never knew existed.

CHAPTER 4

We survived the winter because of the Quakers. My da was a proud man, but my ma wouldn't let Da's pride get in the way of the survival of her children. There were too many days when Da would bring nothing home and even Danny couldn't find anything of value.

Ma would force Da to swallow his pride and we'd take the long walk to Skibbereen. My legs became so tired. I couldn't keep up with my family. Ma would linger behind with me. When we fell too far behind, Da came back. I braced for his harsh voice, but he surprised me. He didn't say anything. He lifted me and swung me up on his shoulders. He carried me the rest of the way to Skibbereen. I don't know where he found the strength.

There was a tall stone building by the river in Skibbereen. Hundreds of people stood in line waiting to get into the building. We joined the line. Da set me down and I stood beside him. A soft rain was falling and I started to shiver. Ma leaned over and wrapped me in her arms.

It was finally our turn and we entered the warmth of the shelter. I'll never forget the smell. When so many people are so close together in a room, they stink. There were rows and rows of wooden tables and more people than I could count sat on the benches. Each person had a bowl, a spoon, and soup.

It was real soup with real vegetables and even a little bit of meat. I never saw Danny eat so fast. He licked the bottom of his bowl when he was finished.

The Quakers brought the cauldrons to Ireland. My da said the Quakers shamed the English into opening the soup kitchens. I don't know if that's true, but I know without the soup, I may not have survived.

We could not dawdle because there were too many people waiting for our seats. We had a most wonderful surprise when we left the shelter. A kind woman stood at the doorway and as we left, she gave us a piece of bread. It was still warm from the oven. I can still taste it.

Since we were in Skibbereen, I knew Ma would not let us go home without stopping at our church. The statue of St. Patrick stood by the doorway as if to welcome us inside. Da would not go into the church with us. The church had a different smell. I could smell the incense left over from Mass. It was a soothing smell. We all knelt in a pew near the altar. Ma led us in the rosary. Danny prayed, but his mind seemed to be elsewhere. Suddenly, I became so tired. Maybe it was because my stomach was full. I knew that I shouldn't, but I crawled up on the pew and laid down. I fell asleep.

CHAPTER 5

When you don't have food, all you think about is food.

I wonder if I stopped growing during the time of the famine. Danny grew. I could tell because his pants kept getting higher and higher on his calves. But my pants, Danny's old pants, still rubbed the top of my feet. When Danny stood by our mother, he was now taller than her.

I remember when we were little, Danny and I would always fight. But when Paddy left, Danny changed. It was like he didn't want to fight anymore. I'd catch him staring at me. He had our ma's eyes. Like hers, when he looked at me, his eyes seemed full of worry.

Spring came and the fields were muddy. There were days when I was just too tired to go scrounge in the fields. Ma would let me stay home by myself. I'd spend most of the day just lying in bed sleeping. Sometimes, I would wake crying. I don't know why I cried.

I remember one day, Danny came home before our ma and our sisters. I was sleeping and he shook me awake. It took me a while to realize what was different about him. He was smiling. It had been so long since I saw him smile.

"Sit up," he said.

I swung my feet to the floor. He pushed me the rest of the way up. He lifted his cap from the side of our bed. His cap was full of blueberries. I thought, maybe I was dreaming. I didn't want to wake up.

Danny took a berry and slid it between my lips. It was tart and sweet. My brother fed me.

CHAPTER 6

Danny was leaving and I couldn't picture my life without him. Who would I sleep with? How would I ever stay warm?

Uncle Seamus was the bearer of the letter of sad tidings. Paddy and Caitlin arrived safe in America. Caitlin had promised her little sister that once they were settled, she would send money to pay for her crossing. Paddy had a job with Uncle Richard and Caitlin cared for an old lady. They took the money they saved and sent it with the letter to pay for Brigid's passage. There was also money for Danny to go with Brigid to America.

We were all to go to the ship to bid Danny farewell, but Mary threw a hissy. I think she was mad because she wanted to go in Danny's place. She felt it was her right because she was the oldest, but Danny was the oldest boy. Mary stayed home and sulked. Joanna didn't want her to be alone, so she stayed home with her.

I don't know how Brigid's da got hold of a cart and donkey, but he did. Brigid was too small to walk all the way to where the ships were, so she rode in the back of the cart. When I got tired, I rode with her. She wanted to play, but I was too sad.

Danny walked by our da. I thought he would be happy to go to America, but he seemed sad like me. Sometimes, he'd come back and walk by the cart. He wouldn't talk but just stare at me and his eyes would fill with that worried look.

My ma and Brigid's ma walked behind the cart. Ever so often, Aunt Sarah would stop and my ma would go over and hold her. I don't think Aunt Sarah wanted Brigid to see her crying.

We finally made it to the ships. Uncle Seamus was waiting for us. To me all the ships looked alike. I don't know why Uncle Seamus chose one ship over another. Uncle Seamus went into the ship and came back with a man and woman. Francis and Julia were young. Like Paddy and Caitlin they were newly married. They were to watch over Danny and Brigid on their crossing to America.

And then my life changed. We were all gathered on the wharf. Danny came to me to say his goodbye. I was crying. Danny lifted my chin and stared into my eyes.

He said, "Michael will go and I will stay."

My da shouted, "No!"

Danny pushed me in front of our da and said, "There's only death for him here. If he goes to America, he'll live."

I took my brother's place on the ship to America.

The Crossing
1848

CHAPTER 1

I was heartsick when I left my family. I cried all the time. Julia tried to comfort me, but she wasn't my ma. The rocking of the ship made my stomach hurt and I couldn't keep anything in it. Eventually, I got used to the ship's rocking and my stomach settled.

For Brigid it was a game. She thought that she was just going to visit her sister and then she would come back home to her ma and da. She had no concept of time or of how long the voyage would take.

The ship stank and the smell would only get worse the longer we stayed on the ship. At home we could always go outside to do our business, but we couldn't leave the hold at night or during stormy weather. We had to use a bucket. At the far end of the ship, an old woman had hung a blanket from the ceiling and the women would go behind the blanket to use their buckets.

The ship was huge. There were more people in the ship than there were in the soup kitchen. Next to the wall, there were like two large beds that ran all the way down the ship. They were up off the floor and one bed was above the other. Everyone slept together. Francis slept with Julia in his arms and Julia slept with Brigid in her arms. There was no one to hold me, so I was always cold.

The ship was damp and dim. We had feeble light from whale oil lamps that hung from the ceiling. There was a large wooden table in the middle of the room. Men would sit at the table and talk. Women and children would stay in their beds. Julia would tell us stories of her family back home, but the stories would only make me cry.

We ate oatmeal every day. It was always cold and the water they used to make it gave the oatmeal a bitter taste.

If we had stormy weather, the captain would make us blow out the lamps and they would shut the hatches. It would be so dark. I don't know what Danny would have done. He didn't like the dark. Everyone prayed for the storm to pass.

One day, when the ship wasn't rocking as much as usual, Francis took me up on deck. It was so strange to see the sun. The ocean went on forever. The ship's sails looked like white clouds. We didn't stay on deck too long. I started to shiver because the wind was so cold.

I must have slept a lot because I don't remember much about the endless days of our crossing. But I'll always remember the night when I woke up and everyone was screaming.

Chapter 2

I thought I was having a nightmare. It was dark and everyone was screaming. I covered my ears, but I could still hear the screams. There was a faint light that came from the open hold above the stairway. People were fighting their way up the stairs.

"Francis, what's happening?" shouted Julia. Her voice scared me because she sounded so afraid.

Francis climbed out of our bed. He grabbed and lifted me, but I slipped out his arms. My feet didn't land on the floor, but in water. I had never felt anything so cold. Francis pulled me up. I wrapped my arms around his neck as tight as I could. I felt his heart pounding against my chest.

"We're sinking," Francis said. "We've got to get out of here. Get Brigid."

Julia scrambled out of bed and scooped Brigid into her arms.

"Come with me," Francis shouted.

"What about our things?"

"Leave them! We need to go! Now!"

We joined the mass of people moving toward the light. I felt Francis stumble, but because there were so many people around us he didn't fall.

Bigger men shoved smaller people out of their way. It seemed like it took forever until we reached the stairs. Everyone was squeezed together. Julia and Brigid were right behind us. I reached back over Francis's shoulder and held Brigid's hand.

We came up into moonlight. We followed the others across the tilting deck. It looked like a white mountain was right in front of our ship. The sky above the mountain was filled with endless stars.

We stopped. There was no place left to go. A wall of people huddled in front of us. The ship creaked and moaned and kept tilting. Everyone seemed so afraid.

The sun was rising and its light gleamed off the ice mountain. Francis forced our way to the end of the deck. I could see near the front of the ship people were sliding down ropes to the ice below, but there were so many people and only a few ropes.

There was a loud crack. The ship shuddered and the deck heaved. A man behind us shouted, "Jump, Jump for God's sake or we'll all die!"

Passengers started leaping from the deck to the ice below. There were horrible screams as they hit the ice. Some people quickly got up. Many did not.

"Michael," Francis said. He pulled my arms from his neck and stood me on the deck. "I'll go first. I'll catch you."

I don't know how far it was, but it seemed like such a long way to the ice. Before I could say anything, Francis turned and jumped. He sailed through the air. He hit the ice and his feet slid out beneath him. He landed on his back. He turned to his side and then tried to push up. But before he could stand, someone behind me lifted me and threw me into the air. I remember the feeling of flying.

It must have only been seconds. I remember flailing my arms as if they were wings. My feet hit first and then my knees buckled. I rolled forward and flipped onto my back. I opened my mouth to scream but I couldn't draw a breath.

Francis stood over me. Suddenly, I gasped. Frigid air filled my lungs. I coughed. There was a loud crack like the snap of a whip.

I heard someone scream, "Francis!"

I looked to the ship. Julia stood on the edge of the deck with Brigid in her arms. Francis ran to them.

CHAPTER 3

I tried to move, but it was like my body didn't want to. My toes and fingers tingled. My breath came out like fog. I watched Francis run to the ship. He ran around people lying on the ice. A few Irish stopped and tried to help the passengers who were hurt, but many just ran away from the ship.

Francis made it to the boat. Julia grabbed both of Brigid's hands and dangled her over the edge of the ship. She swung the child away from the boat and then let her go. Francis caught Brigid and they both fell to the ice.

There was another loud crack and more screams. I saw Julia jump.

A face appeared above me. "Are you hurt?"

I thought it was Danny. I blinked. It wasn't Danny, but a boy not much older. I had seen him before. He played with the older boys on the other side of the ship.

"We've got to get away from the ship or the ship will take us down with her," he said.

He grabbed my arms and pulled me to my feet. My knees buckled, but he held me up.

"Come on." He lifted my arm over his shoulder. I tried to get my legs to work.

There were people around us. One man was crawling, dragging his leg behind him. I could see a white bone sticking out from his bloody trousers. There was another loud crack and the ice shook. We turned around. The front of the ship rose up in the air. People were sliding down the deck. Everyone was screaming. And then the ship just slid into the water.

The ice beneath us shook so hard that we both fell to the ground. All around us it sounded like someone was cracking a whip. The ice before us suddenly split open. The Irish who were there just disappeared. The man with the broken leg fell into the crevice. Water washed up to fill the cracks in the ice.

The boy sprang to his feet. I tried to get up, but before I could, the boy yanked my collar and pulled me behind him like I was a sled. He ran across the ice.

The shaking stopped. The boy stumbled and fell. His face was white and his eyes were wide with terror. I looked back to where we came from. The ice had split apart. Many of the passengers from the ship stood on a mass of white ice across a gulf of blue water. I thought my eyes were playing tricks, but the people on the ice seemed to be getting smaller. I realized they were drifting away from us.

Screams came from the ones who fell in the water. The screams didn't last long.

I was able to stand. I limped toward the water. The boy's hand on my shoulder stopped me.

I screamed, "Brigid."

I lifted my hand to shield the sun from my eyes. I searched to try and find Brigid, but there were so many people and they were drifting farther and farther away.

Chapter 4

A distraught man ran by us. He stopped at the edge of the ice. He screamed, "Emily!" He held his arms out imploringly as he stared across the chasm between him and the iceberg. He yanked his hair. Suddenly, he jumped into the ocean. He tried to swim, but his arms just thrashed. The water was so clear that I could see his face as he sank. He seemed to be screaming.

The iceberg continued to drift away.

The passengers that were left with us on our white mountain gathered together at the edge of the water. Some threw their arms around one another and wept with joy upon finding a loved one. Others, like one woman, collapsed and held her arms to her chest. She rocked back and forth and wailed.

Few were dressed to be outside in the frigid air. Most wore the clothes that they slept in. I was one of the lucky few who had a coat. I was always cold, so I slept with my coat on. Like many others, I wore no shoes, but at least I had wool socks that my ma had knitted for me.

The sun rose higher in the startling blue sky. It was so bright that it hurt my eyes to look at the snow.

"You're shivering," the boy said.

My teeth were chattering. "I'm cold."

The boy tilted his face up to the sun. "We're lucky it's spring. If it was winter, we'd probably be frozen by now." His stomped his shoes upon the ice. He had good shoes. I was jealous.

"What's your name?" he asked.

"Michael."

"I'm Cormac."

I kept my cold hands in my coat's pockets. My feet were bitter cold from standing on ice. I took turns standing on one foot and then the other.

Cormac surveyed the land around us. "There's nothing to build a fire with."

"Where is your family?" I asked.

He seemed surprised by the question.

"In Ireland. My da sold our pig to send me to America. I'm supposed to get a job and send money back home for their crossing."

"The other boys you played with, they're not your brothers?"

"They're just blokes like me. What about you? You're too little to be by yourself."

"Francis and Julia are watching over Brigid and me. We're on our way to live with my brother, Paddy, and Brigid's sister, Caitlin, in Philadelphia.

"Don't cry. Your tears will freeze."

I didn't even know I was crying.

"How old are you?"

"I'm 8. I'm just little for my age."

He pointed to the iceberg that was getting farther and farther away. "There are a lot of people over there. I'm sure your family is OK."

CHAPTER 5

The sun rose higher in the sky, but it didn't seem to give us any warmth.

I kept shivering. I tried to ask through my chattering teeth, "What are we going to do?"

Cormac held his bare hands in the shelter of his armpits. "I don't know," he shook his head and said forlornly, "I don't know."

I counted. There were 20 of us left on the ice mountain. I was the only child. One man kept walking in a circle. He was talking to himself. Most of the other passengers had gathered in a group away from the water's edge.

"Your lips are blue," Cormac said.

I tried to feel my lips, but my fingertips were numb.

"We've got to get your feet off the ice." Cormac walked over to me. He turned his back and squatted down. "Climb up."

I swung my arms around his neck. Cormac stood. He pulled my legs next to his stomach.

"Your feet are like blocks of ice."

He slid his hands into my woolen socks. I could barely feel his fingers squeezing my feet. I rested my head on Cormac's shoulder. He walked us toward the people gathered together.

The Irish had huddled tightly together for warmth. It was hard to tell where one body stopped and the next began.

As we approached, a man about my father's age said, "Put the boys in the middle."

A path opened and Cormac walked through it. Women were in the center of the circle. The circle closed. Bodies pressed against us. I felt warm breath on my neck and hands rubbing my back. Out of the wind, it wasn't as cold.

The man who let us in said, "With no shelter, we won't survive the night."

The woman behind me responded, "We're in the Good Lord's hands. His will be done."

I was suddenly tired. My eyes closed and I fell asleep.

I awoke with a jolt of pain. Numbness had fled my fingers and toes and now they felt like they were on fire. Needles of hurt shot up my legs and arms. But I had a more urgent pain.

"Are you OK?" Cormac asked.

I was still on his back and our faces were almost touching.

I whispered, "I've got to pee."

"You have to hold it."

"I can't."

Cormac said loud enough for everyone to hear, "The boy needs to pee." He pushed our way out of the circle. We walked a little way away from the others. We had our back to them and we faced the ocean. Cormac squatted and I slipped off his back.

"Let's get to it. I might as well join you," Cormac said.

I fumbled with my trousers. Cormac was already out and peeing. His strong, yellow stream stained the snow. He was so much bigger than me. I barely got my trousers open before I let loose. I checked to see if Cormac was watching, but he was looking out at the ocean. Suddenly, he buttoned his trousers and ran forward. He stopped at the water's edge.

He waved his arms above his head and screamed, "A ship!"

CHAPTER 6

Those who were able ran toward the water. Men and women stopped near the edge of the ice. They screamed and waved their hands above their heads. Some of the women were crying. Those who couldn't run limped after us. We all stood on the edge of the ice. We swung our arms in the blue sky and prayed the ship would see us.

Our prayers were met with the sound of cracking whips.

A man shouted, "Get back!"

Cormac grabbed my arm and we ran. I slipped, but Cormac wouldn't let me fall. I heard screams, but I didn't glance back. We ran.

The cracking stopped. Cormac stopped and I stopped with him. We turned and looked back. There were cracks in the ice and streams of water sparkled in the sunlight. Cormac's chest heaved. Some of the passengers were still limping across the ice toward us, but the rest had made it to the safety on the higher ground and thicker ice.

Cormac looked at me. He started laughing. I knew he was laughing because we once again cheated death. He kept laughing and I laughed with him.

We could see the ship's sails, but I couldn't tell if the ship was getting closer.

"If only we had something to make a fire," Cormac said. He kicked the ice and glanced around. "But we have nothing." He looked toward the sky. "We won't have the sun too much longer."

I started to shiver.

"You better get back up."

He turned and squatted and I climbed up.

"It's a good thing that you're light as a feather." He curled my feet around his stomach and slid his hands into my socks. "Plus you help to keep my hands warm."

I squeezed him and snuggled my face into his neck.

A big man who had a long white beard and a bald head came and stood by us.

He pointed to the ship. "Look, boys," he said. "You've got young eyes. Is the ship getting closer?"

Cormac shifted me higher on his back and said, "I think so."

I stared at the ship then closed my eyes and counted to 20. I opened my eyes. "The ship is getting closer. I'm sure."

"Praise The Lord. If only they can get here before dark."

Twilight came. We were all too tired to continue to wave at the ship. We huddled together, but now everyone stood so that they could each see the ship. Some of the women were praying the rosary. The sun was setting behind us.

They lit torches on the ship. I followed the flames as the ship came for us. And then the ship stopped and would come no closer.

CHAPTER 7

The sun set. The stars came out. Never had I seen so many stars. I stared at the sky in wonder. The air was crisp and frigid. Cormac's body warmed me.

"What are they doing?" the bald man asked.

We studied the ship. It looked like torches were moving down the side of the ship and then the flames seemed as if they were floating on top of the water.

Cormac said, "A boat is coming for us."

There were a few gasps, and sighs and murmured prayers of thanks from the Irish around us.

The old, bald man said for all to hear, "We have to go to the boat, but we have to spread out so that the ice doesn't crack beneath us. I'll go first. Keep in one line behind me. Whatever you do, don't bunch together." He started carefully walking across the ice to the approaching flaming torches.

"Should I get down," I asked.

"No, your feet will freeze. Together, we don't weigh as much as him." Cormac started after the man.

We had only gone a little way when the man slipped and fell. I squeezed Cormac while waiting for the whip crack of breaking ice, but all I heard was the wind. The man slowly pushed himself up and stood. His legs shook. He continued walking on.

Cormac took small steps across the slick spot where the man fell.

"We're lucky the sun set," he said.

"Why?"

"Because the ice has refrozen. We should be all right."

I don't know if it was the ice or the wind that moaned. We traveled on. The closer we came to the water's edge, the more afraid I became.

The boat was almost to the ice. I looked back. The line of Irish looked like ghosts walking through the starlight.

The boat bumped up against the ice.

The old, bald man shouted to the sailors, "Be careful lest the ice gives way beneath you." He moved slowly to the boat.

The sailors used their oars to keep the boat next to the ice. One sailor stood. He had one foot on the ice and one foot in the boat. I held my breath as the old man waddled like a duck toward him. The ice moaned. The sailor helped him over the gunwale. Another sailor helped the old man to the back of the boat.

"Get down, Michael."

Cormac squatted and I slid from his back.

"You go first." He pushed me ahead.

I shook my head. I grabbed his hand. "No, you come with me." I threw his words back at him. "We don't weight as much as the old man." I wouldn't let go of his hand. I wouldn't leave him. I pulled and my friend followed. I felt the ice creaking beneath us.

The sailor lifted and swung me into the boat. Cormac jumped in after me. A gust of wind and then a wave rocked the boat.

The next passenger in line didn't wait. He ran to the boat and quickly scrambled aboard and then all the other Irish started running to the boat.

The old man screamed, "No." But the passengers wouldn't stop. The sailor tried to help them into the boat but he could only help one at a time. The others kept coming. They piled up on the ice.

It sounded like gunshots and then the roar of a cannon. The ice shook and heaved and then started breaking apart. The sailor fell back into the boat. Some of the passengers slipped and fell into the opening cracks. A man jumped from the shaking ice. His hands caught the gunwale. A sailor helped to pull him aboard.

The boat drifted away from the ice and the screams. A few of the Irish jumped into the water. The sailors used their oars as lifelines. A lucky few managed to grab ahold of the oars and the sailors pulled them into the boat.

It happened so fast and then it ended so quickly. The Irish were gone from the ice. A few heads bobbed in the water and then the sea took them.

I turned and hid my head against Cormac's chest. He put his arms around me. He held me as the boat rocked beneath us.

CHAPTER 8

A sailor lifted a torch above the two men who had jumped in the water. They looked like icicles. Their hair and beards were coated with ice. Even their eyebrows were frozen. They sat on the bench and shivered. There was no way to get them warm. No dry clothes for them to change into. The sailor just shook his head. He put his torch in the holder built into the gunwale and took up his oar.

The old man stood and glared. He shook his fist at the Irish in the boat. "You should have listened to me," he shouted. "The others would still be alive if you had only waited like I told you." The fury left him. He collapsed on the bench and stared at the ice mountain.

I huddled in Cormac's warmth.

There were six sailors in the boat and they all rowed together. Two of the sailors sat facing Cormac and me. They leaned back and forth as they dipped and pulled the oars through the water.

"How could you find us?" Cormac asked. "The ocean's so big. How could you find us?"

The sailor stared at Cormac and said, "All ships follow the same currents and winds across the ocean. It's like we all travel on the same road that goes from Ireland to America. We have to keep a sharp lookout for other ships and especially now for icebergs." He nodded to the sailor rowing next to him. "Griffin's got the best eyes. You're lucky he was standing watch."

"I saw the iceberg." Griffin said. "I shouted down to the captain. He saw you through his spyglass."

"You're lucky it was daytime," the other sailor said. "We wouldn't have seen you in the dark."

"What ship were you on?" Griffin asked.

I didn't know the name of our ship.

"The Hannah," Cormac whispered as if he was afraid to say the name out loud.

The sailors nodded and rowed in silence.

I turned. I could no longer see the ice mountain behind us. I turned back and watched as the torches on our ship of rescue came closer. The flames danced before my eyes.

I thought of Brigid and Francis and Julia. I wondered if they'd be waiting for me on the ship.

"The others?" I asked. "What about the others?"

"What others?" Griffin asked.

"Some of the other passengers were on another part of the ice that broke away when the ship sank," Cormac said. "They drifted away from us."

"I saw no one else," Griffin said.

I felt like Griffin slapped me. I started to cry and then I started to sob.

"Maybe another ship picked them up," Griffin said consolingly.

Cormac pulled me close and held me as I sobbed.

CHAPTER 9

We sat in silence as the sailors rowed to our ship of rescue.

The ship loomed over us. Stars disappeared in the torch's bright lights. Sailors threw a net over the side and we climbed up. My knees shook. I was afraid to look down. Afraid my hands would slip and I would fall into the frigid water. Cormac was below me and when I'd pause, he'd push my butt upward. When I got to the top, a sailor lifted me over the gunwale.

The ship was much smaller than the Hannah. Sailors and a few passengers had gathered on the deck. They stared at us. I felt like I was some strange animal that they pulled up from the ocean. A woman came forward and wrapped a blanket around me. Cormac stood by my side.

A man shouted from the quarterdeck, "Take them below and give them some food."

He must have been the captain because Griffin led us below. It was warmer out of the wind. Griffin took us to the galley. We sat at a large scarred, wooden table. The cook dished out warm stew with real meat and bread. I thought I was dreaming. Cormac quickly spooned the stew into his mouth. I don't even think that he chewed the meat. I was surprised when he finished that the cook gave him another bowl. We never got another bowl on the Hannah.

I looked around the galley. There were only eight of us at the table – six men and two women. The man across from me, his ears and nose were black. I wondered if mine were too. I didn't see the two men they pulled from the water. I never saw them again.

We finished eating. I just wanted to put my head down on the table and sleep.

The ship wasn't like the Hannah. It was built to carry cargo, not people. They sent our two women to sleep in the cabins that were shared by the few passengers the ship carried. They sent the men to sleep with the crew. They didn't know what to do with Cormac and me. Finally, they sent us to sleep in the room where the cook slept.

The room was right next to the galley. It was small and stuffy and smelled of flour. There were two bunks, one built atop the other. The top bunk was empty. That was where the cook slept. The bottom bunk was covered with bags of grain. Cormac helped the cook move the bags into the galley. I just stood and watched.

When they finished, Cormac climbed into the bottom bunk and I climbed in after him. The cook left and shut the door. Weak light glowed through the cracks in the doorway. I was so tired, but I couldn't sleep. We lay on our backs side by side. I stared through the dim light at the slats of the bunk above us. I was cold. I snuggled closer to Cormac to try and steal his warmth. He rolled to his side and I rolled to mine. I pushed back against his stomach. He put his arm around me. I felt his breath on my neck. He warmed me. I fell asleep.

CHAPTER 10

I awoke to voices. It took me awhile to realize where I was in the dim light. I reached for Cormac, but he was gone. I don't know how long I slept. I sat on the edge of the bunk and listened to the voices, but I couldn't make out the words. I stood. My toes hurt, but the pain wasn't as bad as before. I opened the door and walked out into the light.

Sailors were gathered around the table. Their voices stopped and they stared at me. I looked down to avoid their eyes.

"Sit here, boy," the cook said.

He set a plate with two biscuits covered with gravy on the table. As he leaned forward, I saw Cormac behind the cook. My friend was cutting vegetables on a wooden board. I could feel the smile on my face at the sight of him. Cormac smiled back.

I took my seat. The men towered over me. They seemed so big and strong. They smelled. Their scent reminded me of how my da would smell when he came home after a day working outside in the fields. It was a man's scent. My ma would never smell like that.

As I reached for the biscuits, I noticed my filthy hands. I should have washed them. I turned them over. It wasn't dirt. My fingers looked blue – almost purple. They hurt when I closed my hand. It felt like needles were pricking my fingers.

The cook set a mug in front of me.

"It's tea. It will warm you."

I nodded my thanks. The sailors started talking again. It was hard to understand them. The used the same words we did, but the words sounded different coming out of their mouths. Some of the words they used I had never heard before. The whole time they talked, I could feel their eyes upon me.

The ship's bell clanged and clanged. The sailors grumbled. They stood and jostled each other as they left the small galley. I looked around the table. I couldn't believe what I saw. The sailors had left some food on their plates. In Ireland, no one ever left food on their plates.

I finished my biscuits. The cook put me to work. He had me wash the plates and mugs. Cormac kept cutting vegetables. If the cook wasn't looking, he'd pop a cut carrot into his mouth. When the cutting board was full, he slid the vegetables into a big pot.

As a reward for our work, the cook gave us each a hardtack biscuit and sent us up to the deck to get some fresh air.

CHAPTER 11

The sails were full and the ocean was calm. The boat glided across the small waves. The sun felt warm on my face. I looked up. Griffin was high up in the crow's nest. I waved at him, but he didn't see me. The captain was on his quarterdeck. He had his spyglass trained out to sea. I looked where he was staring. The white sails of a faraway ship seemed to be floating into the blue horizon.

We went exploring. A couple of the sailors were swabbing the deck. One sailor sat on a barrel. He sewed a sail. He bit the end of thread off with his teeth. There were sailors aloft in the rigging.

"Come on," Cormac said.

He ran and jumped. He scampered up the rigging. Higher and higher he went. For him it was a game. He had no fear. He waved for me to join him, but my feet wouldn't move.

The old, bald man stood alone in the front of the ship. He held onto the gunwale and stared at the horizon. I went and stood next to him. The ocean seemed endless. The old man seemed wise. I hoped he had the answer I wanted.

My voice timid, I asked, "Do you think another ship saved the others?"

He leaned down and put his hand gently on my shoulder. He had kind blue eyes.

"It's spring and there are ships coming from Ireland and many more ships coming from Liverpool in England. The weather's been calm. I think another ship would have seen them, and if they saw them they would have rescued them."

His words gave me comfort

"Who are you missing?" he asked.

"Brigid." I sighed. "And Francis and Julia, who were watching over us."

"Brigid's your sister?"

I shook my head. "No. She's Caitlin's sister. Caitlin and my brother Paddy are married. We were on our way to stay with them in Philadelphia. Danny said I was to watch over Brigid. He said she's family now."

"Danny?"

He's my other brother. He made me come in his place. He would have taken care of Brigid, but I didn't."

"Don't cry. It's not your fault. You're just a child. There was nothing you could do." He squeezed my shoulder. "I'm sure Brigid's alive and worrying about you just like you're worrying about her."

I wiped my nose on my sleeve. "Do you really think so?"

"I do."

I don't know why I believed him, but I did.

Chapter 12

They were happy days and I didn't want them to end. When I thought about Brigid, I knew she was safe so I put her in the back of my mind. The ocean was calm. We had the sun during the day and stars at night.

For the first time in my life, I had more food than I could eat. The cook kept us busy. He told us his name was Ian. He was the only man on the ship who had a big stomach and the only man who seemed to always smile. I think he liked to cook and to have his own galley.

I washed the dishes and scrubbed the table and floor. Cormac helped Leo with the dicing. He had a knack for the knife. Cormac pestered the cook with questions about spices and which ingredients to add to the pot. Ian was patient with my friend and soon he was giving Cormac more and more things to do.

We got to know all the sailors. They'd come down before they'd start their watch and come back when the watch was finished. If it wasn't time for a meal, they'd come for coffee and hardtack. The captain wouldn't allow liquor on his ship, so the sailors drank a lot of coffee. Cormac would drink coffee with them and listen to their every word. The sailors would spin their yarns, each one trying to outdo the other. If they talked about women, Cormac's face would turn red. He'd laugh along with them, but I didn't understand their jokes.

We'd spend our breaks topside. Cormac loved to climb the rigging. A sailor said Cormac was like a little monkey.

And that's what they started to call him. I don't think Cormac minded.

One day, my friend climbed all the way up to Griffin in the crow's nest. I don't know how he could be so brave. He smiled in triumph and waved down at me. I waved back. We both knew that I was too scared to join him.

At night, we'd lie in our bunk and talk in the dark. Cormac didn't seem to miss his family as much as I missed mine. He said his da was mean, especially if he got ahold of some poteen. More than once, Cormac said he felt his da's fury. He was glad to be rid of him, but he worried about his ma and his sisters. Two of his older brothers had already left for America. They haven't heard from them since they left. His younger brother died from the fever. Cormac didn't know why he didn't catch the fever like his brother. He didn't know why his brother died and he lived. As he told his story, I wondered if all families in Ireland shared the same tales of woe.

We slept like two spoons pressed together. His arm was around me. I liked being held. I liked his warmth and the way he made me feel safe.

Chapter 13

Cormac grew to love life on the sea, but I never did. I missed the feel of solid ground beneath my feet and the smell of the earth. I wanted to sleep on a bed that wasn't rocking. I wanted to live in a solid house that had a warm fire.

On the ship, I could look across the water at the distant horizon, but I could never look straight down at the water beneath the ship. I was too afraid I'd see the bodies of fallen Irish rising from the deep. They wanted me to join them. I needed to get far away from the place of my nightmares.

The crew was in high spirits at breakfast. They talked only about New York and how much they would drink and the girls they would visit. There was none of the usual grumbling as they left the galley.

I knew our voyage was coming to an end. What would become of me?

We were left to our chores. I finished first and waited topside for my friend. The wind had perked up and the waves were rough. Clouds swirled above the sails. The air smelled different. There was a ship far in front of us and one following behind. Cormac joined me. He had found his sea legs, but I never did. I walked with one hand clutching the gunwale. Cormac bounced lightly on his feet next to me.

Cormac seemed different. He seemed happy.

"Do you know anyone in New York?" I asked my friend.

"Not a soul."

"What are you going to do?"

Cormac beamed. He had the most beautiful smile. "I'm going to stay on the ship." He jumped and scampered up the rigging.

I was speechless. I didn't understand what he was saying.

Cormac shouted, "Ian offered me a job. I'm to be his helper." He swung so that he was facing back toward Ireland. He shook his fist and screamed, "I'll never go hungry again."

CHAPTER 14

We heard a shout of, "Land Ho." Footsteps raced across the deck above us. We scampered up the steps to join the others. It was just a smudge of darkness on the horizon, but it was land. Passengers came out of their quarters and joined the crew. The sails above our heads seemed to be filled with a huge sigh of relief. One man danced a jig. Everyone laughed, but me.

I was sick with dread. Cormac could stay on the ship, but I knew I was too young and too little. The captain would keep Cormac, but not me. And I had family I needed to be with. Paddy and Caitlin were waiting for me. I had to find Brigid. I knew I couldn't stay with Cormac and he wouldn't come with me. I didn't know what to do. I didn't want to leave my friend.

The crew was busy. We knew to stay out of their way. There were other ships around us. We were all headed to the same harbor. There were sailing ships like ours, but also ships made of iron that belched smoke into the air. Cormac said they were steamships that didn't rely on the wind. He said one day all the sailing ships would disappear. I thought that was sad because sailing ships are so beautiful as they glide over the ocean.

Closer and closer we came to land.

I was surrounded by shouts from the crew. Bells clanged and horns blasted as we entered the harbor. The air grew foul and then stank like a privy. My stomach twisted with worry. I leaned over the gunwale and lost my breakfast. Cormac stood by me and rubbed my back.

I gagged again, but there was nothing left. I spit and wiped my mouth with my sleeve. My legs felt weak.

Cormac's eyes filled with concern. We knew we would have to part, but neither of us wanted to leave the other.

"I'll hide you on the ship," Cormac said. "I'll bring you food. When we're back at sea you can come out. The captain will have to let you stay, at least until we reach another port."

"And then what will you do?"

Cormac blew out a breath. "I don't know." He wrung his hands. "What else can we do?"

I felt as sorry for my friend as I felt for myself. Cormac knew I wanted to stay with him. But there was nothing we could do.

CHAPTER 15

It was a warm day and the sun was high in the sky when we made landfall. I hadn't eaten anything because my stomach was too nervous. Cormac hovered by me. He'd look at me, but I would look away. I couldn't bear the thought of leaving him. I didn't want him to see me cry.

We stood on the deck. The ship was tied to the wharf. I had never felt smaller or more afraid in my life. Everywhere I looked, there were buildings, but even in the sunlight they seemed dark. And people. I had never seen so many people gathered in one place. Many had faces that were different colors and the wind carried voices I couldn't understand. I couldn't bear the thought of leaving the safety of the ship.

Ian came up and got Cormac. He had chores for Cormac, but none for me. The voyage was over and I was no longer under the cook's care. I know Cormac didn't want to, but he left me.

I had never felt more alone than at that moment. I stood on the deck. The world spun around me. My legs started to shake. I felt like I couldn't breathe.

"Michael."

I heard my name. I thought I must be dreaming.

"Michael!"

I looked down at the wharf. A man was waving at me.

I tried to get my mouth to work, but no words came out. All I could do was lift my hand.

I waved at my brother.

Chapter 16

It felt so much like a dream. My brother ran up the gangway and then across the ship. And then I was in his arms. I squeezed him so tight. Of course, I cried.

"Easy now, Michael."

Paddy peeled me off of him. He pushed me away and stared at me.

"I've found you at last. Brigid said that I would. I've met every ship that has come into the harbor in the last three days. Now you're here."

I stuttered, "Brigid."

"She's safe. She's with her sister. I sent her home on the train with Caitlin. She needs rest and so does Caitlin. The baby will be coming soon."

It was too much too fast. My knees buckled. I sat on the deck. Paddy knelt in front of me.

"You'll be OK. I'll get you home. It'll just take time to get your bearings."

Now that our reunion was real, I couldn't meet my brother's eyes. Paddy didn't know the guilt that I carried across the ocean.

I looked down at the deck and said, "I didn't ask to take Danny's place. I know you wanted him to come, not me."

Paddy's large hand gently lifted my chin. "Oh, Michael, I wanted you both to come, but I only had money enough for one. I chose Danny because he is older. I wanted you here just as much as Danny."

He stood and then pulled me to my feet. "Danny wanted you to take his place. That was his choice. I'm just so glad that you are here and safe."

My brother put his arm around my shoulder and led me across the deck. We got to the gangway, but I couldn't leave without saying goodbye.

"Wait, I need to say goodbye to my friend. Can you come with me?"

"Of course I can."

Cormac sat on the bench in the galley. He was peeling potatoes. He looked up at me and then he looked higher up at my brother.

Cormac laughed as he realized who stood beside me. "And I thought I was the lucky one."

"I don't know how he found me, but he did. This is my brother, Paddy."

Cormac smiled at Paddy. He tossed me the potato. "There are plenty of potatoes here in America. Neither of us should ever go hungry again."

I didn't know how to say goodbye. I wanted to go and hug my friend. I wanted to feel his arms around me. I wanted to smell his scent and feel his body pressed against mine. But even at my young age, I knew some feelings between boys belong in the dark.

"You're off then," Cormac said.

I shrugged.

"You'll have a grand life in America."

I nodded. I felt my brother's hand on my shoulder. I knew it was time to leave. We got to the doorway. I stopped. I turned back to my friend.

"Thank you for helping me."

It was Cormac's turn to shrug. He smiled. He had the most beautiful smile.

He was my first love.

PHILADELPHIA

CHAPTER 1

We lived in Philadelphia, but only for a few years.

Paddy's first child was named Joseph Thomas after my da and Caitlin's da. The second boy was named Thomas Joseph. The first girl was named Margaret, but we called her Maggie just like my da called my ma. Three children in four years, Paddy kept himself busy making babies when he wasn't working with my uncle in the shop. Somehow, Caitlin kept her beauty. She was like a mother to me.

My brother sent me to school. He said we needed a scholar in the family. I liked school. I liked it very much. I was always the smallest boy in my class, but I was the smartest. I didn't like to roughhouse with the other boys. At recess, I'd much rather stay in the classroom and read a book. The older boys never picked on me like they teased the other smaller boys. They knew my brother was the blacksmith. Paddy was tall and strong. If I put both my hands around his forearm, my fingers would barely touch.

Caitlin was always trying to fatten me up, but it didn't work. There were other small Irish boys like me in our school. I think the famine stunted us. We never grew as tall nor as strong as the boys who were raised in America. Paddy was lucky because he left before we started to starve. I wonder what my life would have been like if I had left with him.

Brigid was small like me. Her skin was bone white and her eyes ocean blue. She was like a second mother for the wee ones. When we'd get home from school, she'd care for them as Caitlin cooked our meals. Brigid had a way with children. She told me she couldn't wait to have her own. She said as soon as she turned 15, she would marry me. I laughed and said a brother couldn't marry his sister. She said we both knew I wasn't really her brother.

Caitlin didn't like Philadelphia. We stayed with Uncle Richard and Aunt Biddy in their home next to the blacksmith shop. Their children were all grown and gone, but the house never felt big enough for all of us. Caitlin said we were country folk and didn't belong in the city. She didn't like the constant noise; the incessant hammering coming from the shop, the loud voices of customers, the neighing and whinnying of the horses. She wanted the peace and quiet of a country life. When she looked out her widow, she wanted to see the sun rise over open fields.

Caitlin wasn't like my ma with her rosary always entwined around her fingers, but she would make us say grace before meals. On Sundays, she insisted that we all go to Mass at St. Michael's.

Caitlin said we couldn't go to Mass unless we were clean. On Saturday night, I'd soak in the tub for my once a week bath while Paddy would do his once a week shave. He told me Caitlin didn't like the feel of a beard when she pressed her cheek against his. She said it made her itch, so to keep her happy he would shave every Saturday night.

The shop wouldn't open on Sunday. We'd dress up in the clothes that Caitlin had sewn for us. It wasn't like back home in Ireland where everyone went barefoot. We all wore stockings and shoes.

We'd parade down the street in our finest. Brigid would always carry the littlest one. She would beam so much that you would think that it was her own child. Paddy and Caitlin would carry the toddlers. Caitlin didn't want them to stumble and get their clothes dirty.

Mass was long like it was in Ireland. The words were the same. Latin is Latin no matter where you go. St Michael's was grander than our St. Patrick's back home. The smell of incense was the same, but not of people. In America, people smell cleaner. I wonder if they all took their Saturday baths.

I always felt closest to my ma when I was in church. Sometimes, I'd turn and expect to see her sitting next to me with her fingers moving over the beads of her rosary.

CHAPTER 2

The famine weighed heavy on everyone's minds.

St. Michael's was not an Irish church. It was built down by the docks. It was a three-block walk from Uncle Richard's house. Inside the church, I would hear English, but also German and Polish and Gaelic.

I remember the first time Paddy and Caitlin took Brigid and me to church and introduced us to Father Wagner. He smiled, but his face seemed so sad as he looked at us.

At Mass, after he finished his sermon, Father Wagner asked Brigid and me to come and stand near him on the altar. I didn't want to go, but Paddy pushed me. Our Pastor said that Brigid and I were living proof of why the parishioners needed to open their hearts and purses to help the destitute Irish. I was shy. I stared at my new shoes that hurt my feet. I couldn't see her, but I'm sure Brigid looked like a small angel.

Caitlin told me that that Sunday, St. Michael's sent the parish's largest donation for famine relief to Ireland.

After Mass it was time to catch up on what little news we heard from Ireland. We'd go to the school hall for coffee and donuts. The limit was two donuts per child except for me and Brigid. We could have as many donuts as we wanted.

The Irish were clannish. We'd gather in the north end of the hall away from the others and talk would turn to home. Like Paddy and me, so many of the Irish had loved ones they left behind. News of death in Ireland traveled slowly, if at all. Letters were treasured and meant to be shared because so many Irish families were entwined. If a new letter arrived during the week, the person who received the letter would bring the letter to the hall. Most of the Irish couldn't read. Caitlin became our reader. I'd study her eyes and face as she scanned the letter. I would know before she would open her mouth whether it was good news or bad.

I think it was very hard for Caitlin to be the bearer of so many tales of woe.

After we left the hall, we'd have our Sunday dinner. I'd sit by the fire and read as Aunt Biddy and Caitlin made our food. Sometimes, Thomas would toddle over and crawl up on my lap. He liked to be held and tickled. He was a happy child and he thrived under Caitlin's care. I wasn't used to being around little ones. In Ireland when the famine came, women stopped having babies. The few who were born didn't live.

The aroma of the food cooking in the kitchen would drive me crazy. I'd find myself drooling as much as the baby. When dinner was served, we'd all gather around the large wooden table by the fireplace. There were chairs for all of us except for Maggie, who would lie in her crib. Uncle Richard had made high, wooden chairs for his own children, and now Joseph and Thomas sat in their places at the table.

Uncle Richard would carve the ham. Aunt Biddy would ladle food on all of the children's plates. We'd bow our heads as Uncle Richard said grace.

I'd close my eyes and think of Da and Ma, my sisters, and, of course Danny. I'd remember us all sitting in the soup kitchen, Da with his swallowed pride, Ma praying over her bowl of soup, my waiflike sisters with dirty faces and dressed in clothes that were no better than rags. I'd think of Danny who would give me his only slice of bread.

Grace would end and I would look at my American family and the bountiful table before us.

They didn't understand why I was crying.

CHAPTER 3

Back home in Ireland, gossip was the national pastime. Few people knew how to read and still fewer knew how to write. News was spread from the lips of one person to the ears of another. In our small clachan, a good story told in the morning would have reached everyone before they climbed into bed at night.

That all changed with the potato famine and the black fever. Our neighbors who didn't flee to America or to the workhouse kept to themselves. No one wanted the black fever to come knocking on their door.

News of the families left behind in Ireland was hard to come by. The only way we could learn about our families was through letters, but letters took time. A letter sent from America would take weeks to reach Ireland. A letter sent from Ireland could take months to cross the ocean. And then there were the letters like the ones lost on the Hannah that would never be read.

But that didn't stop Caitlin. After Sunday dinner, she'd linger at the table with her pen and paper. She'd write her letter home. She'd send it off with a prayer. Sometimes, months later, her prayer would be answered and a cherished letter would come from her ma.

It was a letter that Caitlin sent from Philadelphia that changed Brigid's and my life. The words and money in a simple, well-worn, white envelope brought us from Ireland to America.

After we arrived, Caitlin sent one letter after another to her mother with the glad tidings of our safe crossing. Weeks passed and then months and then years without a reply. Each day that passed, Caitlin became more disheartened. She didn't know what to think. We heard stories of entire villages that were wiped out by the fever. There was no one left to tell their story.

Caitlin said that the not knowing if her family was safe was driving her crazy. Paddy told her that if anyone knew the fate of their families it would be Uncle Seamus. Caitlin wrote him a letter. Paddy put some money inside the envelope that he had saved for Danny's crossing.

Caitlin sent the letter and the money off with a prayer. She is still waiting. We never received another letter from Ireland.

CHAPTER 4

As I grew stronger, Uncle Richard and Paddy gave me more chores to do. I liked being in the shop. No matter the weather, it was always hot in the shop. Especially on winter mornings, I liked to stand in front of the forge. The heat would drive the chill from my bones.

Sometimes, I'd glance at Uncle Richard and think he was my da. They both had thick red beards with gleaming high foreheads. Uncle Richard wasn't a hard man like my da. He had a ready laugh. He liked a good joke and he would pass the joke along from one customer to the next. He'd laugh along with them as he told the same joke over and over.

Life as a blacksmith made Uncle Richard and Paddy strong. Their arms seemed like they should have been on a bigger body. Paddy towered over me. Back home he was a hard worker. Here he seemed driven to work even harder. He never seemed to get tired and he never complained.

I could watch my brother for hours. He'd hammer the red hot iron until it took on the shape of his choosing. I loved the sound of the hiss that the iron made when he submerged it into the water bucket and the way the steam rose like smoke. But Paddy wouldn't let me near the forge when he was working. He showed me the scars from healed burns on his wrists and he'd shoo me away.

After school, my job was to clean the stalls of the horses waiting to be shod. The horses weren't like our horses back home. These were beasts. They seemed twice the size of any horse I ever saw in Ireland. Paddy said they weren't bred for speed but for work. Their job was to pull the carts and wagons. The horses' immense size scared me, but their eyes were gentle. I soon found that they were deceiving. They weren't beasts; they were as gentle as their eyes.

I'd muck the stalls, but I wanted to do more. Uncle Richard would send me on errands. I'd run to the mercantile shop to pick up small parts that were needed or to tell Mr. McCloskey to deliver the parts in his cart if they were too big to carry. Sometimes, Uncle Richard gave me too many things at one time. I couldn't remember them all, so I would write them down in my school notebook. My uncle would stand over me and study the words that I wrote. He'd nod and smile his perplexed grin, but I knew he couldn't read the words I wrote and neither could Paddy.

I wanted more and more responsibilities. The shop was always busy. Sometimes it was too busy. It was my job to run and let the customers know when their horses were ready so that they could come and get their horses and pay their bill. Sometimes, they'd come right away, but many times they'd wait and come the next morning. There were days we'd have too many horses and not enough room for all of them to spend the night.

I asked Uncle Richard, "Instead of having the customers come get their horses, why don't I just take the horses to them?"

He looked at me and laughed.

I tried to be serious. "I can do it and I can collect the money they owe while I'm there."

When he realized I wasn't joking, he scratched his beard and studied me. He raised his thick eyebrows and said to Paddy, "What do you think?"

"He does get along well with the horses. The O'Mearas' mare is shod and ready to go. Give him a try."

I felt butterflies in my stomach.

"You're sure you can do this?" asked Uncle Richard.

I walked over to the mare and stroked the white streak above her muzzle. She whinnied. I looked into her eyes. "You're a good girl, aren't you?" She settled under my touch. I took the bridle and led her from the stall.

It must have been quite a sight. The mare's withers were higher than the top of my head.

My uncle laughed. "You're not going to ride her, are you? It would take a ladder to get you up there."

"No. I'm just going to walk her home."

Paddy took an apple from a basket that hung on the wall. He handed me the apple. I fed it to the horse, being careful of my fingers

Uncle Richard joined us. He attached horse blinders to the bridle. "You don't want her to get distracted. Wagon horses are used to the blinders."

I led the mare and she followed me out into the sunshine.

CHAPTER 5

Caitlin didn't like the city, but I did. After I would deliver a horse, I'd take my time walking back to the shop. The city always felt so alive, so colorful and so noisy. Countless stores lined the street and it seemed like each store carried something different. I'd pause before the glass windows of the shops and let my eyes linger. There were so many things I had never seen before: umbrellas and kites and jewelry.

The city had its own smells; the aroma of leather and sweat from the horses that pulled the carts, the pungent odor of kerosene in the streetlamps, the enticing sweet scent of the bakery.

The city was full of people of all different shapes and sizes. The sidewalks were always crowded. I'd weave my way through the throng. Men with top hats and black coats would walk side-by-side with women in long dresses and colorful bonnets. There'd be farmers who'd come into the city with their boots still mucked with manure and sailors who still smelled of the sea.

I liked to walk behind couples and eavesdrop on their conversations. They wouldn't notice a little boy tailing behind them. I'd learn new words and new expressions. Sometimes, I thought I was learning more on the streets than I was in school.

Back home in Ireland on the farm, I learned about nature. In the city, I learned about people.

I gradually grew. Not with the quick growth spurts of my classmates, but at my own plodding pace. I was still the smallest in my class, but at least I was growing.

Back in Ireland, I would wear Danny's hand-me-downs, but Danny wasn't here. Caitlin was always sewing and knitting. She'd make me clothes that were brand new, not stained and torn. I now wore clothes that fit and were clean. In Ireland, I went barefoot all my life. In America, I always wore shoes with high stockings. I'd have coins in my pockets from the tips people would give me when I returned their horses. I would go into the candy shop and buy my own treats and take home a few for Joseph and Thomas.

I blended in with the others on the sidewalks of Philadelphia. They took me to be one of their own and that was how I felt.

CHAPTER 6

School changed my life. I loved school. I loved learning.
Everything came so easy for me. Aunt Sarah, back in Ireland,
taught me my letters. She gave me a good start. I became an
avid reader at St. Michael's School. Sister Agnes would pick
out books from the library for me to take home.

After dinner, Uncle Richard would have me read him
the newspaper. Paddy and my uncle would sit by the fire. I'd
spread the newspaper out on the table. Words I didn't know,
I would sound out. If my elders didn't know the word either,
I'd write it down in my notebook and asked Sister Agnes at
school the next day what the word meant.

I loved reading, but writing was my downfall. I'm left-
handed. Ever since I was a wee one, I'd always used my left
hand the way my brothers would use their right. That's just
the way I am. My family didn't mind, but the nuns did. They
wouldn't let me use my left hand to write. The first time I
picked up a pen in my left hand, the nun's ruler smacked my
knuckles. It was never natural to use my right hand to write,
but that's what I had to do.

But school in America was more than just letters. I learned
numbers, how to count, how to add and subtract. I could add
up the cost of things that Uncle Richard needed from Mr.
McCloskey's store and tell him how much he would have to
pay. When customers would come in to settle their account,
Uncle Richard would have me add up their bills, collect the
money, and give them their change.

At school, I also learned that I had another talent. Biff McGee was the tallest and strongest boy in our classroom. I think he was a good year older than the rest of us, but no one ever knew for sure. We were all too afraid to ask him his age. At recess, everyone wanted to be on his team. No one wanted to go against him. But Biff struggled in the classroom. He stuttered when he read out loud and he would still use his fingers when he did numbers. But no one would laugh at Biff.

Sister Agnes had me sit next to him. We must have been a sight, the biggest kid sitting next to the littlest. In winter, we only had one recess outside instead of two. We'd use the second recess to work on our homework. Since it was recess, we could talk, as long as we talked quietly. I don't remember if I offered to help him or if Biff asked for my help, but soon we were working together.

Biff was sort of like the horses in Uncle Richard's shop. At first, I thought he was a beast, but as I got to know him, I found that he was just a boy like me. Biff wasn't dumb. He was just one of those kids who needed extra time and help. I would look up and Sister Agnes would be watching us. Sometimes, she would even smile.

I helped Biff with his studies and in return Biff gave me his friendship. For the smallest kid in the class to be friends with the largest was a gift to be treasured.

CHAPTER 7

Very rarely would we have snow in Ireland, but it was nothing like the snow we had in Philadelphia. The storms would come in off the ocean and they could last for days. The wind would howl and shake the glass windows. The house would be smoky from the constant fire in the fireplace. I was always cold.

The bedrooms were upstairs. Uncle Richard and Aunt Biddy shared a room. Caitlin and Paddy shared another with the baby in a crib. All of us kids shared the last room. The toddlers slept in the same bed and I slept in a bed next to them. Brigid had her own bed, but it was on the other side of the room by the window.

The cold wind would bring back the dreams. I'd wake in the middle of the night and Caitlin would be standing over me. She would sit on the bed by my side and hold my hand. I was cold, but I was covered with sweat.

"It was just a dream, Michael," Caitlin said in a voice that she used for the toddlers. She gently stroked my cheek.

I could feel my heart still pounding. "Was I screaming again?"

"It was just a bad dream."

Caitlin might have called it a dream, but for me it was real. I could still see their faces. Across the room, in the dim light from the window, Brigid sat up in her bed. She stared at me. I wondered if she had the same dreams.

When I was calm, Caitlin tiptoed over and checked on the boys. She made sure their covers were snug. She went to Brigid, kissed her sister's cheek, and tucked the blankets around her. She walked to the doorway and then stopped and looked back at us all. She left the door open and went to her room.

I was too scared to go back to sleep. I could still hear the screams and feel the frigid cold. I knew the dead were waiting for me. They wanted to pull me down into the dark water. I lay in bed as rigid as a stone.

On the nights of my nightmares, after all was settled and quiet, I'd hear her soft footsteps. Brigid would lift the covers and slide in bed. She'd snuggle against me and curl her small arm around my stomach and rest her head on my chest. We wouldn't talk, we didn't need to. I don't know if I was giving comfort to her and or if Brigid was comforting me. She'd fall asleep and sometimes, if I was lucky, I too would fall asleep.

CHAPTER 8

Caitlin received a letter, but it wasn't the one she was hoping for. The letter wasn't from Ireland. The crinkled, smudged envelope was from Garryowen, a hamlet halfway across America in the new state of Iowa.

Paddy and Caitlin shared their crossing on the Liberty with Anne and her family. Anne and William weren't bound for the cities like most of the Irish. They wanted to farm just like they did before they were evicted from their farm back home. William had a brother who had land in Iowa. Anne and William were going to join him. They'd stay with William's brother until they saved enough money to buy their own farm. They were told that they could get good land for pennies in Iowa.

In her letter, Anne said their journey was hard and their winters were cold, but the land was bountiful. They now had a farm that was 10 times the size of the land they tilled back home.

Anne said living among the green rolling hills was just like being back in Ireland. Their neighbors were all Irish. Anne said that we should come join them. She said that we could stay with her family while we built our new home.

Caitlin had such a wistful look on her face as she read the letter out loud after our Sunday dinner. I knew her heart longed to be away from the city and out in the country. I knew how she yearned to have her own home.

"We have a life here," Paddy said. "I have a good job. This is our home."

"That's right," said Uncle Richard. "This is your home."

Aunt Biddy added, "I want you to stay."

Caitlin shook her head. Everyone seemed aligned against her – even me.

Paddy said with his voice growing in force, "Michael and Brigid are going to a good school and that's where our children will go when they're older." He pointed to me. "Look at Michael. The boy's got a mind that needs to be nurtured. He's a scholar, not a farmer. The English denied us our right to educate our children. My children will not end up like me. They will go to school." He tapped his finger on the table. "They will know how to read and write."

Caitlin's cheeks flushed as red as her hair. "I can teach the children to read and write."

Paddy snapped, "How can you teach Michael the things you don't know?"

Tears welled in Caitlin's eyes. She stood and ran across the room. She ran up the stairs to her bedroom. The door slammed.

The noise startled Maggie awake. The baby started crying in her crib. Little Thomas joined in and started wailing in his high chair at the table. Brigid cried and ran upstairs to join her sister.

My brother just sat amid the bedlam. He seemed lost, like a child who didn't know what to do.

CHAPTER 9

Caitlin was a formidable woman, especially when she set her mind on something. In the days that followed, she did her wifely and motherly tasks, but without a smile. She talked with Uncle Richard and Aunt Biddy, but she wouldn't talk to Paddy. The house felt as cold as the winter outside. Even the toddlers knew not to cross their mother.

Caitlin and Paddy's bedroom was next to our room. Only the bedroom wall separated my bed from theirs. At night, if I couldn't sleep, I could hear them talking in their bed. I couldn't hear the words. I only could hear the tone of their voices and sometimes laughter.

The voices that I heard now as I lay in bed in the darkness of my room were angry voices. Caitlin might ignore Paddy during the day, but at night she would have her say. Their arguments upset my stomach. I'd lie on my side and cover my ear with my arm. I couldn't fall asleep until they fell silent.

My brother was big and strong, but I knew he was no match for Caitlin. We took our usual baths on Saturday night and Paddy did his weekly shave. That night their arguing ended with their bed squeaking. I knew Caitlin had won. We were going to Garryowen.

Chapter 10

We wouldn't go until the school year ended. Paddy said we couldn't go until the weather was obliging.

I looked up Garryowen on the map in the school library, but it was too small to be listed. I knew it was a tiny town southwest of Dubuque, which sat on the Mississippi River. Paddy said we could take a boat down the coast and then around Florida to New Orleans. We could then take another boat up the Mississippi to Dubuque.

Caitlin said she would never set her foot on another boat that sailed out on the ocean. She said the ocean almost killed her and Paddy and she wouldn't give it another chance. I was so glad that Caitlin had her say because I felt the same way.

Uncle Richard told us to take the railroad at least as far as Chicago and maybe even farther west. When the railroad ended, he said, we could buy a wagon and a couple horses to get us the rest of the way. We'd need the horses anyway to plow the fields in Iowa.

Paddy said we would only take what we could carry. Whatever else we needed, we'd buy in Iowa.

"It's settled then," Caitlin said. "We'll leave at the beginning of summer." She gave Paddy her coy smile. She cupped her hands around her stomach. "That'll be good because the new wee one is due in the fall."

In so many ways, I didn't want to leave. The city grew to be my home. I wanted to stay and go to school. I thought about asking Paddy to let me stay with Uncle Richard and Aunt Biddy, but I didn't. I don't know if it was because I lacked the nerve or if it was because the bond of brotherhood was so strong between us. I knew the journey would be long and Paddy would need my help.

It was hard to say goodbye to Philadelphia. It was harder still to say goodbye to Uncle Richard and Aunt Biddy. Caitlin gave them Anne's address in Iowa and promised that she would write.

I was 14 when we left Philadelphia. It was a sad day, a day full of tears.

TRAINS ACROSS AMERICA

CHAPTER 1

We were lucky. We were traveling in the mid-1850s in the Northeastern part of the United States. We were in the golden age of railroads. We could take the trains all the way from Philadelphia to as far west as Galena, Illinois, which was only 20 miles from Dubuque and the mighty Mississippi River. A decade earlier, we would have had to travel by horse and wagon. That wagon journey would have taken months through the treacherous mountains.

And we had money. Uncle Richard paid Paddy a good wage. He said we were family. He would take nothing for our room and board. Paddy and Caitlin saved their money to bring our families from Ireland to America, but after so many years with no letters from home, they lost hope. The money they saved was now theirs to start a new life.

Paddy couldn't read and I could read much better than Caitlin. It was left for me to plan our journey. Before we left, I learned how to read maps. You couldn't just get on a train in Philadelphia and end up in Chicago. There were so many different railroad lines and different ways to go. There were cities where you needed to get off one train and to get on another. Trains ran on schedules. It was like a game for me. I spent hours trying to find the best way to go from our old home to the new.

Paddy bought me a map, but I knew it wasn't enough. Trains ran on timetables. I needed a watch. When I told Paddy what I needed, he got such a strange look on his face.

He didn't say anything for a while. I felt like he wasn't really with me, like he had gone somewhere else. There was a dim memory in the back of my mind. Years ago, when Paddy and Caitlin left Ireland, I remember our da gave him a pocket watch, but I never saw Paddy wear it.

Caitlin came over and rested her hands on my brother's shoulders. Her touch seemed to bring Paddy back from wherever he had wandered. A strange look passed between them. I don't know what love looks like, but I glimpsed it in the way they stared at each other.

Paddy took me to Mr. McCloskey's shop. Mr. McCloskey didn't have many pocket watches, but he had one that he said the widow of a train conductor asked him to sell. It was silver. When you pressed the top button, the cover sprang open. The polished glass reflected the light coming through the store window. I had to have it.

Paddy had that faraway look again. I offered it to him so that he could hold the watch, but he just gently pushed my hand away. He took money from his pocket and bought the watch.

I was 14 years old and it was my proudest possession. I'd wind it when I awoke in the morning and again before I went to sleep. I'd chain it to my belt and carry the pocket watch with me throughout the day. I was never without it.

CHAPTER 2

We took only what we could carry. We took our clothes and food. We left everything else behind. I think it was hardest on Caitlin. In the days before we left, she'd wander through the house. She'd pick up plates and silverware. She'd just stare at them as if she was trying to memorize what they looked like. She'd caress the highchairs that Uncle Richard made for the boys. She cleaned all our blankets even though we wouldn't take them. Of all the things we left behind, I knew the hardest for Caitlin was the cradle. Her three children had slept in the cradle and now the fourth never would.

Paddy tried to comfort her. He said they came from Ireland with nothing – only the clothes that they wore and not a penny left in their pockets. They would start over, but now they had money and what he couldn't make with his own two hands, they would buy. He would build a new home and a new cradle. His words comforted Caitlin and the thought of a new home brought the fire back to her eyes.

Brigid carried the baby. Caitlin carried our basket of food and kept constant watch over Joseph and Thomas. It was left for Paddy and me to carry the bags. I had two bags to carry. They looked like stuffed pillows. The bags were tied tightly with a rope that connected the top of one bag to the top of the other. I'd lift the rope behind my neck and let it rest atop my shoulders. I carried one bag on each side of me. People would stare at me as I'd waddle from foot to foot down the platform from one train to the next.

Caitlin had sewn a giant bag made out of canvas. It looked like the type of bag that seamen would carry down by the docks. Paddy hoisted the bag up on his back. The weight didn't seem to bother him at all.

One basket of food would not last for our journey. There were places to get food in the stations where we stopped and changed trains, but Caitlin said the food was too expensive. She would always ask me how much time we had until our next train. If there was enough time, she'd have us sit on a bench in the station. I would sit on one end with Brigid on the other. Caitlin would put the boys between us. She'd pile our bags in front of the boys like a barricade. She'd tell the boys if they moved they'd get a spanking, and then she'd add that if they didn't move, she'd bring them back a treat. She'd grab Paddy's hand and they would hustle off to find a market near the station.

They were never gone long, but for me each minute seemed like an hour. I'd constantly look at my watch. I was OK for 10 minutes, but after that I wasn't. I'd be so afraid that they wouldn't come back. At 15 minutes, I would feel my heart start to race. At 20 minutes, it would be hard to breathe and my knees would knock together.

But they always came back.

CHAPTER 3

Our journey kept us going farther and farther from the land of our birth.

The train ride was nothing like our voyage on the Hannah. On the ship, we were confined in a dark hold. On the train, I'd sit by the window. I'd stare out through the glass and it was like a book was opening in front of my eyes. The train would chug along. The pages would turn from scenes of towns to farmlands. The boys would get scared when we entered the dark tunnels that went through the mountains. I remember the thrill of going over a bridge and seeing the deep chasm beneath us. The train would sway around the bends. There was the constant click-click-click of the wheels.

On the Hannah we were always with the same people, but the train was so different. It reminded me of walking the streets of Philadelphia and how people would change from one street to the next. On the train, people would change from one stop to the next. And there were so many stops. Sometimes, it seemed like the train had just started and then it would stop again. The Hannah's voyage was the endless flowing motion of the sea. The train was all fits and stops.

And then there were the smells. On the Hannah, I remember the sulfur smell of the sea and the stink of close-quartered unwashed bodies. On the trains, I remember the scent of burning wood from the fireboxes in the locomotives. Billowing clouds of steam and wood smoke would seep into our clothes and hair.

Caitlin and Paddy would try to keep us all together, which was a hard task. Most of the passenger cars were nothing more than wooden benches. It wasn't easy to find a bench for the seven of us to be together. Joseph and Thomas would do their part to help. One or the other was always crying or fussing. Thomas was going through the terrible twos. His tantrums were a slight to behold. Men who were traveling alone and saw us coming down the aisle would get up and walk to another part of the car.

CHAPTER 4

I'm sure we were quite a slight as we walked the platform from one train to another. Paddy would lead with the large canvas bag hoisted up on his shoulder and our food basket hanging from his hand. Caitlin would follow with Thomas on her hip and a firm grip on Joseph's hand as he walked beside her. Brigid came next with the baby gently caressed against her chest. I brought up the rear with my two swaying bags.

People would stare. Women would come close to try and glimpse the baby in Brigid's arms. Our little Joseph was a showman. He was like a magnet with his blond hair and blue eyes and a smile that dimpled his rosy cheeks. People would stop and gawk as the young boy sauntered by.

But it wasn't all smiles. A few fellow travelers glared at us. Some people would walk around us as if we should be shunned. The way they looked at us made me feel dirty. I'd hear the word papist. I knew the word. The first time I heard the word in Philadelphia, I asked Sister Agnes what it meant. I didn't understand why people didn't like us just because of our religion. I was glad Paddy was with us. I knew no harm would come to us as long as he was there to protect us.

No matter what train we were on, there were always Irish. I read in the newspaper that over one million Irish died and another million came to America during the five long years of the potato famine. The famine ended, but the Irish were still coming. The Irish came to the cities on the coast, but like us, many of the Irish were on the move to the west to seek a better life and fortune.

If we met other Irish on the train, we would sit together. Food would be shared and stories told. One man always seemed to have a flask of whiskey that he would pass around. The stories were all the same. They would start out sad about the loss of loved ones and the heartbreaking beauty of the country we left behind. But the sadness would be replaced by hope. We knew we could have such a better life in America than we had ever known under the thumb of the English in Ireland.

The adults would talk on and on. Joseph would climb up on my lap. We'd sit and look out the window at the fields passing by. The train's rocking and the clickey-clack of wheels hitting the rail joints seemed to sooth the boy. He'd fall asleep. I'd look at the young one in my lap, his golden locks and wonder what sort of life he would have in America.

CHAPTER 5

When Joseph woke up, he had to pee. I took him to the convenience in the back of the train car. It was a small room and only meant for one person. I closed the door. The boy was too little to stand and reach the toilet, so I had to lift him up so that he could do his business. It was hard to stand in one place with the boy in my hands and the train swaying. Joseph sprayed his pee all over the toilet seat.

Joseph's favorite part was to flush the toilet. The flapper would open and deposit our leavings on the track. Joseph would squeal in delight as he saw the wooden ties rushing beneath our feet through the opening. I wondered if people walking the train tracks knew about our offerings beneath their feet.

The train suddenly jolted. I crashed back against the wooden stall and just caught Joseph as he started to fall. It felt like a giant hand was pinning me against the wall. There was a loud, piercing, high-pitched squeal that went on and on. The train slowed and slowed and then came to a shuddering stop.

I took my nephew's hand and opened the door. It was quite a slight. The passengers looked frightened. A woman was holding her kerchief to a girl's forehead. The kerchief was red with blood. The girl must have banged her head against the back of the wooden seat. The floor was littered with loose belongings.

I swung Joseph up into my arms and walked around the scattered bags and books and baskets. I went to check on my family.

We sat for hours. The sun shined through the glass. It was hot and stuffy. We lowered the windows, but there wasn't much of a breeze. No one would tell us why we stopped. No one knew where we were. We were tired of sitting and waiting. Some of the men got off of the train. Paddy and I got off with them.

Around us cornfields seemed to stretch forever. The dark green stalks were taller than me. There must have been a heavy rain because the ground was wet and muddy. Far down the tracks in front of our train, I saw some smoke and a group of men. Some men just stood with their hands in their pockets, but other men seemed to be working on the rails.

We knew the train wouldn't leave while the men were working on the tracks. Paddy took off to see what they were doing. I followed behind him.

CHAPTER 6

I couldn't believe my eyes. A train had fallen off the tracks. The engine was on its side. It looked like an enormous black beast that was struck down. The front of the engine was nosed into the earth. Smoke was rising from the car behind the locomotive that carried the wood that the engine needed to make steam. The wood had caught on fire and was still burning. There were six cars behind the tender and they were all crumpled and smashed. It looked like someone took a giant sledge hammer and went to work. The corn that the train was hauling was scattered amid the corn growing in the field.

We went closer. There were a dozen men working on the rails. They were hard men, all muscles and deeply tanned by the sun. Their clothes looked like they had never been washed. The wind brought us the stink of their bodies and also the musical lilt of Gaelic. It had been so long since I heard my mother tongue that it took me awhile to understand the words.

My brother walked forward and greeted them in Gaelic. The men paused and looked at us.

A man stood off to the side. He didn't carry a pick or a shovel. His tools were a ledger and a pencil. He looked my brother up and down and asked, "Are you looking for work?"

Paddy pointed to our train down the tracks. "We're on our way west. We're going to farm in Iowa. I'm Paddy and this is my younger brother, Michael."

The foreman looked at me and said, "He must be the runt of the litter."

The men laughed. Paddy's face changed. He took on that dark cloud that always hovered near our family.

His voice rising, Paddy said, "You'd be a runt too if you lived through the famine."

The foreman quickly said, "I meant no offense."

Paddy's cloud passed. "None taken."

"From your accent, I take you for a Cork man," the foreman said.

"We're from Carrigillihy. Not far from Skibbereen. I left before it got bad. Michael didn't. He came later."

I felt the men's eyes on me, I looked at my feet.

"You're not going anywhere until we get these tracks fixed," the foreman said. "We have an extra shovel. I can pay you good coins for your labor."

"I've been cramped up in a box for days. My body needs the work. I'll take the coins. Give me a shovel."

CHAPTER 7

Paddy joined the others. My brother never minded getting his hands dirty. Set a task before him and he wouldn't stop until it was finished. He fit right in with the other men. They all had broad shoulders and thick forearms. They talked as they worked. In the midst of the Gaelic, I felt like I was back in Ireland.

I didn't know what to do so I just stood and watched. The foreman came over and stood by me.

I pointed to the engine, "What happened?"

"Too much rain. They should have put more stones under the tracks, but they didn't. The rain softened the earth. The rails buckled under the engine's weight."

"Was anyone hurt?"

"The engineer broke his arm." He stared at the smoke rising from the tender. "The fireman wasn't as lucky." He made the sign of the cross on the front of his body and so did I. "It was lucky that the train was hauling freight and not people. Who knows how many may have died."

I shuddered.

He handed me his ledger and took a cigar from his coat pocket. He talked out of the side of his mouth as he lit the cigar. "It's a race to see who can set the most tracks. Shoddy work and there are no regulations." The tip of his cigar glowed. "In Camp Hill two trains were on the same track. Neither one knew the other one was there until it was too late. They collided head-on. Over 60 people died and over 100 more were injured. Many of the passengers were horribly burned when the engines exploded." He lowered his voice. "Many of the dead were children on a school picnic." He stared at the smoke rising from the tender.

The foreman flicked the ash off his cigar. He shrugged. "Oh, well. It keeps us busy. We'll just go from one wreck to another until someone finally figures out how to do this right."

"And I thought crossing the ocean was dangerous."

The foreman coughed smoke as he laughed. "If it's your time to go, you'll go." He took his ledger back. "There's no sense worrying about it."

CHAPTER 8

Paddy and the men worked until the sun started to set and still they weren't finished. The foreman told us we'd have to spend the night on the train and hopefully we'd be on our way tomorrow. He paid my brother and sent us off.

Paddy was covered with dirt. His shirt was ripped along the seams. There were half -moon stains under his arms and along his neckline. He had a pungent smell of sweat and earth mixed together. Clods of mud fell off his shoes as we walked the tracks back to our train.

Paddy stretched his arms behind his back. "The work did me good."

"You're quite a sight," I said. "I don't want to be around when Caitlin sees you."

Paddy tried to swipe dirt stains from his pants.

"Your clothes are ruined." I sniffed. "And you're pretty ripe." I laughed. "You won't be sleeping next to Caitlin tonight."

I ducked as he tried to thump the back of my head with his dirty palm. I danced away.

He laughed and shouted at me, "I can clean the shoes. I made enough money to buy all new clothes and still have some left over to buy something nice for Caitlin. You've got a lot to learn about women."

I laughed and shrugged. I eased back to his side. We walked the tracks together.

We returned to a party. The farmer, who owned the field, told the waylaid passengers that they were welcome to take as much corn from his field as they could eat. Fires were burning along the train tracks and corn was roasting.

Caitlin's face was a sight to behold when she laid eyes on her husband. A look of concern quickly changed into a flash of anger as she realized Paddy wasn't hurt.

Paddy held his hands up defensively as he walked toward his wife.

I saw the boys gathered around a fire with Brigid. I left my brother to fend for himself. I ran off to join my nephews.

CHAPTER 9

The setting sun sent streaks of pinks and violets shooting across the sky above the cornfield. Like everyone else, I ate until I was stuffed. I walked away from the fire. I sat on the stones of the railroad embankment and watched the boys as they played tag in the twilight of the cornfield. There was no breeze, and the air was stifling.

I sat and thought how different life was in America. Here, children like Joseph and Thomas were healthy and thriving. They had never cried themselves to sleep while going to bed hungry. In Ireland, the landlords took our corn while we were starving. Here in America, a farmer who I didn't even know freely fed us from his bounty.

"You look so sad," said Brigid. She sat down next to me so close that our legs were touching.

I didn't answer. I just watched the boys.

"Sometimes the sadness just comes," she said softly. "I don't know what I would do if I didn't have my sister. I miss my ma and da so much and my brothers. Do you think they're all right?"

I didn't want to give her false hope, so I just said what I felt. "It's been too long. I think that if they were all right, we would have heard from them by now."

"I pray for them every night."

"It's good that you do."

"Do you pray for your ma and da?"

"I do and for my sisters and, of course, Danny." I couldn't say my brother's name without choking on the word.

She brightened and said, "I think they're all up in heaven and one day we'll all be together."

It was a nice thought, but I didn't know if it was true.

Thomas shrieked and ran between the cornstalks. Joseph ran behind him.

Brigid stood. "Come on, it's getting dark. We need to get the boys before the banshees come out."

She took my hand. Her hand was warm and soft. She pulled me to my feet. I was still taller than her, but not by much. She had strength that belied her small size. She stared into my eyes. She gave me a look that Caitlin would give Paddy. I wondered when she got so grown up. I wondered what happened to the child I used to know.

Chapter 10

Even with the windows down, it was too hot to sleep in the train car. We went outside. It was too muddy to sleep in the field, so we spread our coats on the stones of the embankment. It was a gorgeous summer night. There wasn't a cloud in the sky. Stars twinkled above us. The night was filled with chirping crickets. Fireflies danced in the corn.

I slept near the boys. Brigid slept with the baby. Paddy was able to clean himself enough so that Caitlin let him lay with her.

The boys quickly fell asleep as only children can. I was tired, but I couldn't sleep. My mind wandered. Voices of the other passengers hushed around us. The still air brought the sound of a fiddle from the camp of the Irish workers down the tracks.

I could see Uncle Seamus standing by the fire in our cottage with his fiddle under his chin. My sisters, Joanna and Mary, would dance together. Ma would sit at the table and clap her hands. Some nights, Danny would sing as Uncle Seamus fiddled. Ma always said that Danny had the voice of an angel. I heard the melody of "The Minstrel Boy." The song brought my family back to me. It was a song of Ireland, a song of sadness and parting. Whenever Uncle Seamus would fiddle the tune, my da would cry.

My brother, Paddy sat up and hung his head between his knees. Caitlin sat up and hugged him.

I never understood why my da would cry when he heard the song, but now I did.

CHAPTER 11

The sun rose early. It brought us a new day of travel. The tracks were fixed before the sun reached its midpoint in the cloudless cerulean sky. We took our places and the train slowly started to chug-chug. We waved and cheered as we passed the Irish work crew. The workers doffed their hats. One man danced a jig.

We had lost a day, but no matter. We still had the rest of the summer and fall before the weather would change. As long as we would be safe in Garryowen before the first snow fell, we would be OK.

We traveled through the mountains of Pennsylvania. The engine struggled up the steep inclines. Sometimes it went so slow that I thought we could walk faster. The deep woods grew right up to the trackside. I'd point out the deer in the woods to the boys. One time we even saw a bear and her two cubs.

When we reached the top of a mountain, the train would race down the other side. We would all hold tight to our seats as the train swayed through the bends. Joseph and Thomas would laugh while I whispered a prayer. The brakes would squeal and sparks would fly as the brakemen tried to slow our descent.

And then there were the trestle bridges that spanned the deep gorges. I would get dizzy as I gazed down at the miniature world far beneath us.

The train slowed and the woods thinned. Wooden houses and building replaced the tall trees. We came to Pittsburgh.

We never left the station, so I don't really know what the city was like. Pittsburgh was already a major terminal and one of the gateways to the west. It was time for another change of trains and decisions to be made on what trains we would take to Chicago. I studied the maps and timetables. I convinced Paddy and Caitlin to take the northern route to Chicago. We would go up to Cleveland and then along the lake to Toledo and then through the northern farm fields of Indiana.

There were express trains that went faster and didn't stop at all the small towns, but they were more expensive. Caitlin wouldn't pay the extra money for the six of us and the baby. I tried to get her to change her mind. We were all sore and bruised from the constant jostling of the hard wooden seats. It would be quicker and much easier to take the express trains, but Caitlin was the keeper of the purse. She wouldn't part with their hard-earned savings.

So we took the local trains that stopped and stopped and stopped. Sometimes we'd stop in the middle of a field just to pick up a farmer and his wife. We'd have to pull into the sidings to let the express trains pass our train. I'd look at Caitlin and fume as we sat and waited, but she wouldn't look at me.

CHAPTER 12

Pennsylvania reminded me of Ireland with the hills and mountains, but Ohio didn't. Ohio was flat. I'd look out the window and fields would go on and on until they disappeared in the horizon. There were no hills, just miles and miles of flat fields of wheat or corn. No one would ever go hungry in America. There was so much land and so much grain.

I thought of our farm in Ireland. The ground was hilly and rocky and hard to till. We didn't have enough land to plant the amount of grain that we needed to prosper. Our farm, like all the farms around us, was fewer than five acres. The only way we could survive was to plant potatoes. One acre of potatoes could feed us for the year. We planted our acre of potatoes next to the four acres of grain. We sold the grain to pay the rent to the landlord and then lived on the potatoes. We could only survive as long as the potatoes were healthy.

Our world came to an end when the blight came. The landlord still demanded our healthy grain crops to pay the rent. He took our grain and left us with black potatoes.

We had no money to buy food. We never had money. We lived from hand to mouth from one season to the next. Without the potatoes, we knew we would surely starve. When the potatoes turned black, we did.

Anne said in her letter that their farm in Iowa was 250 acres. I can't imagine a farm that big. Their farm was 50 times the size of the one where I grew up. How could one person own so much land? With no landlords to take their grain, the Irish farmers in Garryowen must all be rich.

Caitlin sat in front of me and nursed the baby. She looked out the window and smiled. She nodded at the passing fertile fields. She said that she just wanted her own house on her own farm, but I wondered if she wanted much more.

CHAPTER 13

Traveling was hard. The constant rattling of the train took a toll on all of us. My joints and my teeth hurt.

The boys were cranky and so was I. The wee ones needed to go outside and play. They were too young to be cooped up in the car for hours and hours. They needed to run to get rid of all their pent-up energy. When we stopped, Paddy would take Joseph and I would take Thomas. We'd walk them up and down the station to try and tucker them out.

The toddler, Thomas, refused to sit on the bench. He said his butt hurt. Caitlin pulled his trousers down and took a look. His small oval cheeks were black and blue and cracked from the hard wooden seats. She put ointment on his butt-cheeks. We all took turns letting him sit on our soft laps.

And we smelled. We hadn't had a proper bath since we left Philadelphia. Our clothes desperately needed to be washed. My shirt stuck to my chest and my armpits itched. I wondered if we would ever get the smell of soot out of my coat.

I felt like I hadn't had a proper sleep for weeks. It's hard to sleep sitting up on a wooden bench. I wished I could be like Joseph and curl up on the floor by our feet. The boy could sleep anywhere.

Caitlin said we had to be careful of the water and she was right. At one time or another, we all got the runs. There was only one convenience in our car. There were times when my stomach suddenly cramped. It felt like a hand squeezed my guts. I'd jump up and rush to the bathroom while praying for the door not to be locked.

We finally made it to Cleveland. It was evening and the gas lamps were being lit. The station wasn't as big as Pittsburgh's, but it was still a good size. I checked the board only to find another delay. A boiler on the engine of the train on the tracks to Toledo broke down. They'd have to send a replacement. We couldn't continue our journey until the next day.

Even Caitlin had enough. She couldn't bear another night of sleeping in a train station. Paddy led the way and we carried our belongings from the station down the street to a hotel.

I don't know what I looked forward to most: to soak in a hot bath or sleep in a real bed.

CHAPTER 14

We were worried about the boys. Since we left Cleveland, they just weren't themselves. They both had coughs and constantly wanted water. No matter what their mother offered, they wouldn't eat. Joseph said his throat hurt and Thomas just wanted to be held all the time. Joseph would curl on the floorboards by our feet and sleep. Caitlin was worried and so was I.

We passed from Ohio to Indiana, but no one knew it. The flat scenery didn't change outside our windows. The view was either a field of grain or thick woodlands that one day would be felled to turn into more fields of grain.

The train rumbled along. We made good time. There were no major cities left between us and Chicago. The sun burned hot through the window. The sky was clear. We were all anxious for our journey to come to an end.

Joseph cried and stood up from the floor. He stumbled into the bench. He rubbed at his eyes and cried louder. His eyelids looked like they were glued shut. Yellow discharge coated his eyelashes.

Caitlin quickly handed Maggie to Brigid. She wet her handkerchief with the water bottle. She took Joseph onto her lap and gently cleaned his eyelids. The boy finally opened his eyes. His eyes were bloodshot. He looked at his mother with pink eyes. He said that his eyes burned. His mother gently held the wet handkerchief to his eyes.

Caitlin looked scared.

I held Thomas in my lap. The child was sleeping, but he wasn't in a sound sleep. He'd cough, but his cough wouldn't wake him. I peered down at his angel face. My nephew looked like he was crying, but it wasn't tears that he shed. It was yellow mucus.

I didn't know if I was sick with worry for the boys or if I was really getting sick like them. My throat was sore. It hurt when I swallowed. My whole body ached. Thomas shifted in my arms. I gently wiped the yellow tears from beneath his eyelids. He coughed right into my face.

CHAPTER 15

The train still stopped, but not as often and for not as long. New passengers would get on the train. If they saw the sickly boys, they'd move away to another part of the car, or better yet, to another compartment.

The conductor would make his way through the train. He wore a dark coat with four shiny buttons and a black, round billed cap that had a flat top. He had a grey, bushy mustache. His silver pocket watch chain gleamed against his waistcoat. He'd stop and talk with Paddy. The conductor was Irish like us, but he said he was born in America. He asked about the boys. He seemed as worried as we were.

The conductor told us we were coming up to South Bend. He said that the Priests of the Holy Cross were building a university in nearby Notre Dame. If we were lucky, we might be able to catch a glimpse of the church's steeple.

The train stopped in South Bend. People got off, but no people came into our car. The conductor stood outside and directed the newcomers to other passenger cars.

Thomas coughed and slept. He was heavy in my arms.

Thomas stirred and cried in his sleep. I looked down at his face.

I shouted, "Caitlin."

I'd never seen anything like it. There were red, pimply blotches all over the wee one's face. My shout startled the boy and he woke up screaming. Maggie wailed as her mother tore the baby from her breast and handed her to Brigid. Caitlin quickly came and took Thomas from me. She tried to comfort the boy. Thomas settled under his mother's touch.

Caitlin felt his forehead. "He's burning up."

She wet her handkerchief and patted Thomas' face.

"Paddy, we need more water."

My brother ran off to find the conductor. Joseph moaned and got up from the floor. His face was covered with a red rash just like his brother. His eyes were crusted shut again. He cried and rubbed his eyes. The baby still wailed. Caitlin's eyes darted from one child to another. She seemed like she was being torn apart.

Brigid wet her knuckle and held it against the baby's mouth. Maggie hushed as she sucked the knuckle.

"I've got Joseph," I said.

I took my nephew. Caitlin went to help her remaining child.

I thought Joseph was shaking in my arms, but then I realized that I was the one who was shaking.

CHAPTER 16

Passengers who were still around us took their belongings and fled to another section of the train. Caitlin led Thomas to an empty bench. She laid him on the wooden boards.

Paddy returned with a bucket of water and set it next to Caitlin's feet. The conductor was with him.

The conductor leaned over Thomas and studied his face. He said, "It's just like I feared." He unbuttoned Thomas' shirt. The rash covered the boy's neck and was spreading down his small upper chest.

The conductor sighed, "Well, the devil you know is better than the devil you don't." He looked at Paddy and then Caitlin. "The boys have the measles."

Caitlin collapsed on the bench next to her son. She shook her head in disbelief. "How did they get the measles? We haven't been around anyone who was sick."

"The boys were around someone who was sick," the conductor stated. "They just didn't know it. You can have the measles for days before the rash comes out."

He turned to Paddy. "Have you had the measles?"

Paddy stared at Thomas' face. "I've never seen the likes of this before."

The conductor turned to look at Joseph sleeping in my lap. "Then you'll all get the measles. The disease has already spread from the boys to you." His eyes softened when they fell upon Brigid and the baby. "It's too late to do anything now. The disease is in you."

Paddy asked softly, "But what about you?"

The conductor buttoned Thomas' shirt. "I had the measles when I was about this little one's age. You can only get the measles once. I don't know why, that's just the way it is."

The conductor took out his watch and checked the time. "We'll be in Chicago in a couple of hours. You can stay here until we get to the station, but in Chicago you'll have to get off the train. They won't let you on another train as long as one of you has the rash." He rubbed his fingers across his mustache. "You'll have to find a place to stay. It could be weeks before you're all healthy. None of the hotels in the city will take you. Not with boys the way they are."

"What are we to do?" Caitlin beseeched. She was fighting tears. Her fingers shook against her lips. Her green eyes were wild with fright.

"I have to make my rounds," the conductor said. "I'll be back to check on you." He walked away.

Paddy came and wrapped his arm around her. He said soothingly, "It's OK, Caitlin. It's OK."

Caitlin pushed him away and screamed, "I won't go through it again. I can't. You know what it was like."

Paddy put his hands on his wife's shoulders. He stared into her eyes. "We survived then, Caitlin. We'll survive now."

Chapter 17

Caitlin took turns bathing one boy and then the other with a soft, wet cloth to try and bring down their fevers. They wouldn't eat, but she made them sit up and sip water from the cup. I coughed and her eyes darted to me. My throat hurt when I swallowed. I shrugged away her look. She went back to tending the boys.

Paddy sat on the bench. He seemed in a different world. I wondered what happened in their past to get Caitlin so upset. They never talked about their crossing to America. Maybe they had nightmares of their own.

The clickety-clack of the train went on and on.

The conductor came back. He leaned against the seat as the train slowed. He talked to Paddy, but he stared at Caitlin.

"Bright light will hurt the boys' eyes. Have them wear their hats and not look at the sun. It shouldn't be too bad. The sun will be low on the horizon when we reach the station." He put his hand on Paddy's shoulder. He sounded like a father talking to his son.

"When you get off the train go straight to St. Patrick's Church. It's only a few blocks from the station. Father Dunne is a good man. He's in charge of building St. Patrick's. The church is almost finished. Father Denis will help you. If he can't, he'll find someone who can."

The whistle shrieked as the train came to a crossing. Steel couplings clanked together and brakes squealed as the train slowed. The conductor was like a seaman. The train's changing momentum didn't affect him. Tall wooden buildings lined both sides of the tracks outside the windows.

The conductor left, but he only got a few feet away before he stopped. He turned and came back. His eyes took in Paddy and then Caitlin. The young parents looked like two lost children who had wandered too far from home. Caitlin was doing all she could not to cry.

The conductor's brown eyes filled with concern. He sighed, "Stay here. I'll come back for you. When everyone is gone, I'll help you gather your luggage. I'll get you through the station and help you on your way. Just stay here and wait for me. It'll be a while. I have things I need to do, but I will come back for you."

Light seemed to come back to Caitlin's eyes. "What's your name?" she asked.

"Liam O'Sullivan."

"Thank you. You're a good man, Liam."

"Don't thank me." He touched his chest. "There's a voice inside me that said I have to help you." He laughed. "The voice sounds just like my mother."

He touched his cap and then turned and walked away.

CHICAGO

Chapter 1

The train finally stopped at our station in Chicago. The passengers stood and quickly gathered their belongings. They seemed in a hurry to get away from us. Some of our fellow travelers had to walk near us to get to the exit. They kept as much distance between us and them as they could. They would not look at us as they quickly sneaked by. I knew how the lepers in the Bible must have felt.

It was all hustle and bustle outside our windows in the station, but our car was empty and quiet. Caitlin bathed the boys and held their hands. Brigid sang a soft lullaby to Maggie.

I had no energy. I sat and stared out the window. I knew the sickness was inside me. It was only a matter of time before I would share the boys' fate. In people's eyes, I would become a leper like my nephews. What would become of us?

I was tired, just so tired. All I wanted to do was sleep. I closed my eyes and leaned my head against the window.

The rap of knuckles on the glass woke me. It took me a second to get my bearings. The conductor stood outside the window. He had a two-wheel-cart filled with our baggage. It had gone dark and quiet outside. The gas lamps were lit in the station. He motioned us to come out.

I turned to Paddy and said, "Mr. O'Sullivan is here." The voice I heard didn't sound at all like mine. It was dry and raspy. It hurt to say the few words.

Caitlin buttoned up the boys. Paddy gathered our things. Brigid put a bonnet on the baby. I stood. The world was spinning. I held onto the seat until the dizziness passed.

Paddy scooped up Joseph. Caitlin lifted Thomas. I stumbled over and went to lift our carry-on bag. As I lifted the bag, my knees gave out. I fell to the floor. I was more embarrassed than hurt. I used the seat to pull myself up.

"Michael, you're white as a ghost," said Caitlin.

I went to lift the bag again.

Paddy pushed my hand away and said, "I got it." He shifted Joseph higher on his shoulder and held him with one hand. With his other powerful hand, he easily lifted the bag.

"Can you walk?" he asked.

I nodded that I could even though I wasn't sure.

Chapter 2

The station was eerie in the lamplight. The big black beasts weren't bellowing their clouds of smoke. There were no shouts of "all aboard" or clanging bells or high-pitched steam whistles. The trains were sleeping and wouldn't wake until the next morning. The few people walking or sitting on the benches seemed like ghosts.

I held onto the side of the cart as Mr. O'Sullivan wheeled it through the station. Brigid walked beside me. Maggie slept in her arms. Paddy and Caitlin were behind us. The boys would lift their heads off their parents' shoulders and glance around.

We left the station. We came out to a broad wooden sidewalk and a wide street. Beside the street lamps, there were lights glowing through glass windows from the shops lining the avenue. The day's heat was still with us. There was a slight breeze that carried the sound of music and laughter. The breeze chilled me.

A horse and wagon were waiting for us. The driver got down and helped Mr. O'Sullivan load our luggage into the wagon. Paddy tossed our carry-on over the side. He slid Joseph into the wagon and then took Thomas from Caitlin and set him by his brother. Caitlin went aboard next. Brigid gave her the baby and then climbed in after her. As I tried to climb up, my knees gave out again. Paddy lifted and swung me into the wagon as if I weighed nothing.

"This is Aidan," said the conductor to Paddy. "He'll get

you to the rectory. He's had the measles so you don't need to worry about him."

The conductor reached into his vest and pulled out a coin. He gave it to Aidan. He turned to Paddy and said, "I best be on my way or the Missus will think I stopped at O'Malley's pub. I've been known to lift a pint or two."

Paddy held out his hand. "I can't thank you enough."

Liam shook my brother's hand and said, "My ma told me that we live in the shelter of each other. Take care of your children."

The conductor tapped his fingers to his cap at Caitlin and then turned and walked down the sidewalk.

Aidan said to Paddy, "You can ride up top with me."

They climbed up on the bench seat. Aidan lifted the reins and gave them a shake. The horse whinnied and moved forward.

Mr. O'Sullivan disappeared down the sidewalk, but his words have always stayed with me. I looked upon my family huddled in the wagon. Caitlin held the baby. Joseph sat next to Thomas with his arm around his little brother's shoulder. Brigid held my hand in hers. It is in the shelter of each other that we live.

CHAPTER 3

The ride to the rectory was like a dream that I could only remember bits and pieces of. I knew the fever was upon me. I'd go from burning one minute and then shaking with the chills the next. We only went a few blocks, but it seemed a lot longer.

I could see the church. It towered over the street. In the light that lingered after sunset, I could see scaffolds next to the large stone building. The scaffolds went almost to the top of the pitched roof. The rectory looked like a small afterthought next to the enormous church.

Paddy climbed down from the wagon. We waited in the wagon as he went and knocked on the rectory's door. The door opened and he disappeared inside. It wasn't long before he came out. A priest wearing a long black cassock and white collar was with him.

Father Dunne was tall, almost as tall as Paddy. He had a high forehead and thick curly hair that stuck out past his ears. He was clean shaven. He had a mole above his left eyebrow. He was older than Paddy, but not old like my da.

He took a look at all of us and then his eyes settled on me. I was shaking. The chills were upon me. I held my arms tight against my chest.

"Aidan," Father Dunne said. "We need to get them to Mrs. McEneely. She'll know what to do. I'll lead the way." He turned and took off at a fast walk down the street.

My eyes grew heavy, but every time they would close the wagon would hit a rut and bounce me awake. Tall buildings gave way to shorter ones. We stopped in front of a large house that belonged out in the country, not in the city. It had a big well-tended yard. I could hear cows mooing from the barn behind the house.

Father Dunne ran up the porch steps. He pounded on the door, but he didn't wait for an answer. He opened the door and walked inside. He came back with a little woman. She had a hunched back and seemed like a child next to the priest.

Mrs. McEneely peered in the wagon. She had a large nose and deep set blue rheumy eyes. She said, "Bring them inside." She lifted her gnarled hands out to Caitlin, who gave her the baby. Mrs. McEneely pushed back Maggie's bonnet. She lifted the baby to the feeble light.

"On my," she said. Mrs. McEneely ran with the baby to the house.

CHAPTER 4

Paddy lifted Joseph from the wagon and Caitlin took Thomas. I climbed down from the wagon. My knees buckled as my feet touched the ground. Before I could fall, Father Dunne scooped me up in his arms. He carried me to the house. He was strong like Paddy. I remember the smell of him, the aftershave on his neck.

The house was brightly lit with oil lanterns. The pastor carried me through the parlor back to the bedrooms. Caitlin ran out of a bedroom in search of Maggie. Father Dunne took me into the room that Caitlin had just left. There were three single beds, each one set against a different wall. Joseph and Thomas were already in their beds. Paddy stood watch over them.

Father Dunne gently set me in the remaining bed. I was still shaking. The pastor pulled the blankets up and around me. He stared at me with a look of concern. He had eyes like my mother's. He edged the sign of the cross of my forehead with his thumb. He said a prayer.

I fell asleep.

So many things happened over the next couple of days, but I was only awake for part of the time. It was hard for me to know if some things really happened or if I just dreamed them.

I remember a soft cloth rubbing against my eyelids. When I opened my eyes, I saw Brigid. She gently patted the cool cloth against my face, then around my neck and down my chest. I went back to sleep.

I awoke from my nightmares in the middle of the night. My pillow was soaked with sweat. The room was dark. No one came to check on me, so I must not have been screaming. I was too scared to fall back to sleep, but I did.

I awoke with a hand holding the back of my head up. A cup was pressed to my lips. I swallowed and coughed. Mrs. McEneely brought the cup back to my lips. I swallowed again and coughed.

One day, I awoke to prayers. They prayers came from some other room in the house. The prayers went on and on. It didn't matter if the sun was shining or the lamps were lit, I heard the prayers. I thought of my ma kneeling by the fire and praying her rosary. I drifted back to sleep surrounded by prayers.

Screams woke me. It was the worst sound I ever heard. The wails went on and on. I don't know why, but I cried.

CHAPTER 5

I felt a butterfly on my eyelid. I blinked my eyes open.

Joseph pulled his small fingers away from my face. He shouted, "Michael's awake."

Thomas toddled over and stood by his brother. He sucked his thumb and pulled on his right ear.

"You slept for a long time," Joseph said. "Are you better now?"

I took in my surroundings. The drapes were open and sunlight filled the hot and stuffy bedroom. The boys just wore their undergarments. Thomas climbed up on my bed and lay beside me. I studied his face. The red rash had almost completely faded.

My mouth was so dry. I rasped, "Water."

Quick as a flash, Joseph darted across the room. There was a pitcher of water and cups on a nightstand. He filled a cup and brought it to me while being careful not to spill it. I used my elbows to prop myself up. I took the cup and gulped all the water. I gave the empty cup back to Joseph. He went and got me more.

The house was quiet. Through the open windows, I heard people talking and horses and carts moving about on the street.

"Where is everyone?" I asked.

"Mommy and Daddy are sick just like you were. They have their own room. They have the red rash all over their faces. Mrs. McEe said we have to leave them alone so that they can get better."

It took me a moment to realize Mrs. McEe was what the boys called Mrs. McEneely.

"Brigid?" I asked.

"Briggie isn't sick. I don't know where she is. She's been crying ever since Jesus took Maggie up to heaven."

The words numbed me. The prayers and screams were not a dream.

Joseph said, "I'll go find Briggie. Maybe she'll stop crying when she sees you're all better."

Joseph walked away. His little brother got out of bed and waddled after him.

Brigid ran to the doorway. She stopped and looked at me. There was such a look of relief on her face. She quickly came and knelt by the side of my bed. She leaned her head against my chest and sobbed. I didn't know if she was crying for me or for Maggie. I didn't know what to do. I rubbed my hand along her back. Her sobs were enough to break my heart.

She pushed up and tried to gather herself. "Father Dunne says Maggie's in heaven. I believe that's true with all my heart." She swiped her wrist beneath her runny nose. "But I miss her so. I want to hold her, to see her smile. I want to feel her soft touch when she'd curl her little hand around my finger."

I cried. I cried for both Maggie and Brigid.

Brigid wiped the tears from my cheeks. "No, don't you cry. I've cried enough tears for both of us. I know Maggie's in heaven and one day I'll be with her again."

As Brigid looked at me, she seemed to change before my eyes. She straightened and showed an essence of strength that I've glimpsed in her older sister.

"Here I am sobbing when you need my help. You must be starving. I'll get you some soup. Jesus is taking care of Maggie. I'll take care of you."

CHAPTER 6

I managed to sit up in bed. I leaned back against the wall. Brigid sat on a three-legged stool and spooned me warm soup out of a wooden bowl.

It was hard to see the little girl I grew up with in the young woman before me. We were less than a year apart, but in some ways, she seemed older than me. I wish I had eyes as blue as hers and skin as white and pure.

"You didn't get sick?" I asked.

She shook her head. She put the spoon in the empty bowl and set it on the tray that rested on the bed. "I don't know why everyone else got sick, but me. The doctor said …" She gave me a quizzical look. "Do you remember Dr. Ryan?"

I searched my memories, but he wasn't there. I shook my head.

She took a biscuit from the tray and broke off a piece. She handed it to me. The biscuit was warm like her hand.

"Dr. Ryan said some people are immune to the measles. I must be one of them."

She seemed to go away from me and her eyes got teary. "Maggie got the rash. The next day she struggled to breathe and her lips turned blue. Father Dunne went and got the doctor and brought him back for Maggie. Dr. Ryan said the sickness got in Maggie's lungs. He said she had pneumonia. There was nothing he could do. He said all we could do was wait and pray."

I reached and squeezed her hand.

Brigid slowly continued, "Dr. Ryan checked all of us while he was here. Paddy and Caitlin were just coming down with the rash and the fever. The boys were starting to get better." She wrapped both of her hands around mine. "He was worried about you. Your fever was so high. Do you remember Mrs. McEneely and me taking turns bathing you?"

I felt my face flush. I shook my head.

"You were very sick." She turned pensive. "I don't know what I would do if I lost both you and Maggie." She reached for the biscuit and broke off a small piece. Her eyes brightened. "But you're here with me."

She lifted and slid the small piece of biscuit into my mouth. Her fingertips lingered on my lips.

CHAPTER 7

Each day, I grew stronger. My rash disappeared. I would eat anything they'd put in front of me. Joseph bounced back as only a child can. The house seemed too small for him.

I worried about Thomas. He'd tug at his ear and cry. He said his ear hurt. He'd go to his Mrs. McEe and pull on her apron. She would hold him in her lap and press a hot cloth against his ear. That seemed to help the wee one, but only for a while.

Brigid and Mrs. McEneely had their hands full with Paddy and Caitlin, who came down with the measles at the same time. Neither one had the strength to take care of the other. Dr. Ryan said measles was harder on adults than children.

Brigid took me to see them. Even through it was the middle of the day, the drapes were drawn. The dim room smelled like sickness. Paddy and Caitlin lay in bed together. The fever must have been upon them, because they tossed the covers off. Wherever I could see flesh, I saw the red rash.

Mrs. McEneely was bathing Paddy with a cold damp cloth. It was so hard for me to see my brother, who was so strong, look so weak. Caitlin slept beside him. She tossed and turned in her sleep. A strange sound like a rattle came from her chest as she breathed.

A rocking cradle was on the floor next to the bed by Caitlin. I quietly walked to the cradle. Maggie was swaddled in a sheet. I couldn't see the baby, but I knew she was hidden in the white shroud. I set my hand gently on the small bundle.

Brigid came and stood beside me. She whispered, "Father Dunne blessed little Maggie. He said we would have a Mass for the baby when everyone was all better. He said we could bury Maggie in the baby section of the church's cemetery. She'd be with all the other babies that Jesus called to heaven."

Brigid turned to her older sister. "Caitlin said we would have the Mass, but Maggie was going with us. She would not leave her child behind. Maggie would be buried in the church cemetery in Garryowen so that we could visit her after we went to Mass on Sundays." She nodded toward her sister. "You know Caitlin when she has her mind set, no one, not even a priest, is going to change it."

Brigid rocked the cradle as if the baby was only sleeping. "We'll take Maggie with us."

Chapter 8

Father Dunne would come to visit us. He said visiting the sick was part of his job. I grew to like the priest very much. He wasn't holier than thou like some priests who were always preaching the Gospel. We needed help and he helped us.

The boys sat at the kitchen table as they finished their breakfast. I sat with them. The Chicago Tribune was spread out on the table. The newspaper was just as good if not better than the papers back in Philadelphia.

Father Dunne came out from visiting Paddy and Caitlin's bedroom. Mrs. McEneely handed him a cup of coffee.

"They seem to be getting better," Father Dunne said.

"Their fever broke," said Mrs. McEneely. "They're young and strong." She handed the pastor a biscuit. "It's the baby that Caitlin is carrying that I worry about." She gathered the boys' empty bowls. "Only time will tell."

Mrs. McEneely set the bowls in the sink. She came back and stood behind Thomas. "No matter what I do, this child's ear isn't getting any better."

"I'll take him to see Dr. Ryan," said Father Dunne. He looked at me and smiled. "What about you, Michael. Would you like to go with me?"

I couldn't believe he asked me. If he only knew how much I wanted to get out of the house.

I tried to keep the excitement from my voice. "I would."

I walked out the door for the first time since I arrived two weeks before. I felt like a butterfly coming out of a cocoon. I held Thomas' hand. We walked beside Father Dunne along the wooden sidewalk. I no longer felt like a leper.

The street was busy with horses pulling wagons. There was a horse that pulled what looked like a passenger car that you'd see on a train. The horse pulled the car down the middle of the street. The horse would stop and some people would get off while others would board the car.

It was the dog days of summer. The air was dry and hot to breathe. Even the breeze was hot. Everything was dry and dusty. The dust would get in my nose and make me sneeze. It hadn't rained in all the time that we had been in Chicago.

Philadelphia was stone and bricks. Chicago was wood. Everything was made of wood. Buildings were close together, some so close they were almost touching.

Thomas stopped and pointed. I looked where he pointed. I couldn't believe my eyes. A house was moving. It was coming toward us down the street.

CHAPTER 9

Father Dunne stopped and looked back at us and then he looked where we were staring. He laughed.

"It's quite a sight, isn't it? You don't see moving houses in other cities."

He pointed to a group of men working down across the street. I don't know how they did it, but the men were lifting a building up off the ground.

"Chicago was built on a marsh," Father Dunne said. "In spring, if you try to go down this street, the mud will be up to your knees. But we're not going to leave our city. We need the lake and the port that comes with it. So we have to lift our buildings up out of the dirt. Our only choice is to make the ground higher and put sewers in the ground to drain the water back to the rivers and the lake." He pointed across the street. "Some buildings we can just lift and fill the dirt beneath them." He turned to the moving house. "Others we have to move and resettle somewhere else."

The house kept coming toward us. A team of horses pulled a large flat wagon. The house rested on wooden beams that extended over the sides of the wagon. A man and woman were inside the house. They stood in the doorway and waved at us.

Thomas squealed with delight. He wiggled his small fingers at the couple. I laughed and waved as the house went by.

"Chicago is a grand city," said Father Dunne. "And it's only going to get grander. We Irish built the Illinois and Michigan Canal. Now, anything that comes across the lake to

Chicago can be shipped by barge all the way down the rivers to New Orleans."

Father Dunne took his handkerchief and wiped his sweaty forehead. "You came by trains. Just like you, the trains are bringing hundreds of Irish to Chicago every day. There's work here for any Irishman who's not afraid to get his hands dirty. The trains not only bring us people, they bring goods from the east and farmers' grain and cattlemen's livestock from the west. One day, trains will travel from the Northeast on the Atlantic Ocean all the way to where the sun sets on the Pacific. All those trains that cross America will go through Chicago."

He shoved his handkerchief back in his pocket. "Chicago has no choice but to become the grandest city in the heart of America. It will be the gateway between the east and the west. And the Irish will build this city and live here. You walk the streets of Chicago today and one out of every five men that you'll meet is Irish. More Irish are coming every day."

Chapter 10

We probably would have got to the doctor much quicker, but Father Dunne had to stop and talk to everyone we met. Most of the people were Irish, but some weren't. Once he stopped, he had a hard time getting away, especially from the old ladies who just wanted to gab.

We went to Dr. Ryan's house. He didn't have an office like some doctors. He worked right out of his home. Mrs. Ryan met us at the door. She was about the same age as my ma. She wore a white apron and her hair was pinned up above her neck. She led us into the parlor. There were a half-dozen people sitting on chairs and waiting. A boy my age had his arm in a sling. His mother sat next to him. A man across from us had a swollen crooked nose and black eyes. He must have been on the wrong end of a fight.

Mrs. Ryan took us past the other patients to a room off the hallway. She asked Father Dunne if he would like some coffee. The priest just shook his head. She said Dr. Ryan would be with us shortly.

The walls of the room were lined with shelves and the shelves were filled with books. It was just like a library. I couldn't help myself. I walked to the shelves and looked at the books. Most of the books were about medicine, but some were novels. Dr. Ryan had one of my favorite books, *The Deerslayer* and another, *Moby Dick*, that looked brand new.

It wasn't long before Dr. Ryan came in and I reluctantly had to leave the books.

"What brings you here, Denis?" asked Dr. Ryan.

I couldn't believe he didn't call him Father Dunne.

The priest pushed Thomas forward and said, "This little one's ear isn't getting any better."

"Let's have a look." Dr. Ryan lifted Thomas and set him on the table, which was in the middle of the room. The table was covered by a white sheet.

Dr. Ryan slid open a drawer built into the table. He took out a small weird instrument. He said softly to Thomas, "I need you to sit still so I can take a look in your ears."

I went and stood next to my nephew. Dr. Ryan peered into Thomas's left ear and then into his right.

"Just like I thought, the right ear is infected." He said to Father Denis, "I need to poke a hole in his eardrum and drain the infection."

Thomas didn't understand what the doctor said, but I did.

CHAPTER 11

Dr. Ryan said to Father Denis, "You'll have to hold him still." His voice turned serious. "You can't let him move."

"Wait." I put my hand on my nephew's small shoulder. "I'll do it. He knows me."

I looked at the toddler and said, "Tommy, I'm tired. Let's take a little rest. Scoot over. I'm going to lie next to you."

The child moved over and laid down. I climbed up on the table and snuggled next to him. Our faces were almost touching. I put my hand on the side of his head. My fingers played with his curls.

"Want me to sing a song?"

Tommy nodded.

Dr. Ryan walked across the room and took something from the cabinet. He came back to the table and stood out of view behind Tommy. The doctor looked at me. I could see the long needle in his hand.

I stared into Tommy's eyes and said, "I'll sing the song that my brother Danny would always sing to me."

Dr. Ryan hovered over Tommy. I took a breath and sang softly:

> *"The Minstrel-Boy to the war is gone*
> *In the ranks of death you'll find him;*
> *His father's sword he has girded on,*
> *And his wild harp slung behind him.*
> *'Land of song!' said the warrior-bard,*
> *Tho' all the world betrays thee,*

One sword, at least, thy rights shall guard,
One faithful harp shall praise thee!"

Dr. Ryan nodded. I held Tommy's head still against the table. His eyes widened. He said, "Ouch."

Dr. Ryan pulled the needle away from Tommy's ear.

"We need to turn him on his other side."

"You need to roll over, Tommy," I said. "I'm going to get up and lay on the other side of the table."

I jumped off and ran to the other side. I climbed up on the table. Tommy rolled over to face me. Dr. Ryan lifted the boy's head and placed a white cloth beneath his ear. I set my hand again of the side of Tommy's head and played with his curls.

Dr. Ryan said, "He needs to stay still while the ear drains."

Tommy stared at me. He clutched my hair with his small hand. He looked sleepy. I sang the rest of the song that Danny would sing for our da. Tommy fell asleep before I finished.

CHAPTER 12

Dr. Ryan quietly left the room.

Father Denis whispered, "Danny?"

I stared at Tommy and played with his curls as he slept.

"He should be here instead of me. He sent me in his place. He stayed behind in Ireland with my ma and da and two sisters." I sighed. "We don't know what happened to him or the rest of our family. Caitlin sent one letter after another, but they were never answered."

I turned so that I could see Father Denis. "I live in his shadow. My life was a gift from my brother."

Father Denis moved closer. He had a way about him. I felt like I could tell him things I could tell no one else.

"Danny was so much better than me. He was strong and he was so brave. I could never be as brave as him."

Tears have always been my weakness. Just thinking of Danny brought tears to my eyes.

"Our ma said Danny had the voice of an angel. They would sing together at breakfast. There were happy times, when we were all together, before the famine came."

Father Denis stood over me and said, "The Lord works in mysterious ways. There is a reason you are here and Danny stayed behind. You say your life was a gift from your brother, then use the gift that he gave you. Give your gift value. Use your life to help others."

Tommy stirred. His eyes opened. He smiled when he saw me.

CHAPTER 13

"I'll need to see him in a couple of days," said Dr. Ryan. He walked over to the counter and took a piece of candy from the jar. He handed Tommy the candy. He lifted the boy from the table and set him on the floor.

Tommy showed me the candy. He smiled with delight. I ruffled my nephew's hair.

"What do you say, Tommy?"

"Thank you." He slid the candy into his mouth and held his little right hand out to Dr. Ryan.

The doctor smiled and shook his hand. Dr. Ryan turned to me. "You should be a doctor. You have a good bedside manner."

I shrugged. I didn't understand what he meant by bedside manner.

It was like Dr. Ryan could read my mind. He said, "You understand people and their needs. You put the child at ease. You made it so much easier for me to treat him. Have you ever thought of being a doctor?"

His question took me completely by surprise. "We've always been farmers. We're on our way to Garryowen to buy a farm."

Father Denis said, "We have thousands of Irish who can plow the earth, but very few who can tend to the sick. I've seen you read the paper and I've talked with you. You're a smart lad. Think about your future and how to use your gift."

I mumbled, "I've never thought about it. I always thought I'd be a farmer like my da."

"This isn't Ireland," Dr. Ryan said. "In America you can be anything that you want."

I'm sure I showed my bewilderment.

"Think about it. The Sisters of Mercy have opened a hospital near the river by Rush Street. They need doctors." He nodded to Father Denis. "We take care of our own. We know people. If you want to become a doctor, we can open doors for you."

"Think about it, Michael," said Father Denis. "And pray on it."

CHAPTER 14

I was quiet as we walked back to Mrs. McEneely's house. I had a lot to think about. Dr. Ryan was right, life was different in America. If I would have stayed in Ireland, I have no doubt that I would be a farmer like my da. What choice did I have? We had no books, no teachers. We only had our wandering storytellers. They'd stop and visit and tell stories of the glory of Ireland in the times before the English came.

I feared that going to Garryowen would be like going back to Ireland. Caitlin might want the solitude of a farm, but I didn't. There was so much I wanted to learn. I needed people who could teach me.

We walked on. The buildings and sidewalks on this section of the street were lifted up from the dirt. Tommy walked to the end of the sidewalk. He peered over the edge. He stood a couple of feet above the street. He swung his arms back and forth like he was getting ready to jump.

I quickly grabbed his collar and pulled him back. I gently shook him. "Are you in such a hurry to go back to the doctor?" I took his hand and led him to the stairs.

We came to the intersection of two streets. Down the long street, I could see the blue of the lake and white sails. I wished that I was by myself and that I could just spend the day exploring. There was so much to see, so many new things to discover.

"Do you know how to get to Mrs. McEneely's house from here?" Father Denis asked.

I knew where I was and how to get back. "I do."

"I have other parishioners to visit. I'll leave it to you to get the boy back to his Mrs. McEe."

"I can do that." I blurted out the question that's been in the back of my mind. "Why does she live alone in such a big house?"

Father Denis drew a breath and let it out slowly. "She didn't always live alone." The priest grasped the silver cross that hung from his neck and rested atop his chest. "Cholera swept through the city in 1849. The disease took her whole family, but spared her." His eyes met mine "You never know how someone is going to react to the tragedies that life brings. Mrs. McEneely couldn't save her family, so now she spends her life trying to save others who are in need. She was here for you and your family. Like I said, The Lord works in mysterious ways."

CHAPTER 15

Paddy joined us for breakfast. The boys wouldn't leave him alone. They fought over who could sit on his lap. Paddy had a two-week beard. He was pale. I could faintly see the lingering red blotches. He still had the smell of the sickroom, but that didn't matter to the boys or to me. I was just so glad that he was up and around.

He had an appetite like I had when the fever broke. Mrs. McEneely kept making him pancakes.

"How's Caitlin," I asked.

Paddy chewed and swallowed and took a sip of milk. He hesitated as if he was trying to think of what he should say. He looked at his sons and then at me.

"Her fever has broken …." He stared out the window and seemed to search for the words to go on. "She blames herself. She says we never should have left Philadelphia. She says if we stayed in Philly, Maggie would still be with us."

Mrs. McEneely said in an angry voice, "That's nonsense." Her voice scared the boys. "We have no say over who lives or dies. When the Good Lord wants us, he'll take us no matter where we are." She snatched the boys' empty plates and glared at Paddy. "Caitlin will come to understand God's will, but first you need to give her time to mourn her child. Just let her be and give her time."

Mrs. McEneely spun away from us and angrily shoved the plates into the water. She held onto the counter and stood still as a statue.

Paddy looked chastised. The boys hid behind their father. I could feel Mrs. McEneely's own loss in the words that she had spoken.

Long, quiet, seconds passed and then Mrs. McEneely turned around. She changed into Mrs. McEe and smiled at the boys.

She dried her hands on a towel and said, "Joey and Tommy, we have work to do. The hens have their eggs waiting for us."

The boys came from behind their father. They grabbed their caps from the hooks on the wall and ran to the doorway.

"Paddy," Mrs. McEneely said in a soft voice. "When you're up to it, I have chores for you and Michael. It's time for all you boys to start earning your keep."

CHAPTER 16

I told Mrs. McEneely that I could take Thomas back to the doctor. The boy seemed better. He didn't tug at his ear or cry at night. I felt a thrill when she nodded her OK. Paddy gave me a few coins to give Dr. Ryan and then we were off.

We never had a summer in Ireland like we had that summer in Chicago. The air was so hot that it hurt just to breathe. Women walked the streets with parasols in one hand and fans in the other. They fluttered the fans like bird wings by their faces.

We hadn't gone a block before my shirt was soaked. Everyone moved like it was such a burden just to walk. And then there was the dust. The horses and carts would kick up clouds of dust that would sting my eyes. A water cart came down the street. When it stopped, a line quickly formed. I took Thomas's hand and we joined the line.

Dr. Ryan's office was busy. Father Dunne wasn't with us to speed us through, so we had to wait with the others. There was a box of toys in the corner. Tommy met a new friend and they played with small wooden horses together.

Dr. Ryan seemed happy to see me. He lifted Tommy up on the table and asked as he examined my nephew, "Have you been giving any thought to our last talk?"

I felt like Father Dunne wanted to save my soul, whereas Dr. Ryan wanted to save my mind.

"I have … but I need to help Paddy get our family to Garryowen."

Dr. Ryan studied me and asked, "How old are you?"

"I'm 14."

"You're young. You have plenty of time. Go with your family. Get them settled and then come back."

He walked over to the candy jar and brought a piece of hard candy back for Tommy. He opened his hand. Tommy went to grab the candy, but before he could, Dr. Ryan closed his hand around the treat.

Tommy was shocked. He stared at Dr. Ryan. The doctor smiled and opened his hand again. Tommy quickly snatched the candy. He laughed. Dr. Ryan ruffled the toddler's curly hair.

"The boy's ear is fine," Dr. Ryan said.

He set Tommy on the wooden floor and then walked past me over to the shelf of books. He ran his hand along the books' spines and then took a book from the shelf. He handed me the book.

I turned the book over and read the title *Household Medicine and Surgery* by John Stevenson Bushman.

"A book to get you started on your studies."

Dr. Ryan gave us both a gift that day. Tommy's candy was soon gone, but I savored my gift over a lifetime.

CHAPTER 17

I jolted awake to screams. I thought I was having a nightmare, but the screams were real. A bell clanged and clanged. The bedroom was dark except for an orange glow behind the closed curtains.

Paddy barged through the open door. He screamed, "Get up. Get dressed." He pushed open the curtains and looked out the window. The sky was on fire. Paddy ran to Tommy and started to dress the boy.

I scrambled out of bed. I slid on my shirt and pulled on my trousers. I grabbed my shoes and put them on with no socks. Joseph sat up on his bed. He stared out the window. I saw the fire reflected in his eyes.

I ran to Joseph and helped dress him.

"Come on. Hurry now," Paddy said. His voice was frantic. He swung Tommy up into his arms. He fled from our bedroom. I took Joey's hand and we ran after him.

The front door was open. We ran out of the house. It was pandemonium. Everyone was fleeing their homes and shops. We all gathered on the sidewalk. Mrs. McEneely had her arm around Brigid. The girl was shaking. Her eyes were wide with fright. Caitlin stood by them. She massaged her swollen belly.

Bells clanged. Two men ran down the dark street carrying torches. Behind them came a large hand pumper on wheels being pulled by a half-dozen men. Another half-dozen men were either pushing the pumper or running along the side of the cart. The men all wore hard, red hats. Their breaths huffed like a train as they ran by us.

The horizon was aglow with red flames that streaked to the sky. As I watched, the fire seemed to jump from one building to the next. The wind was so hot. It felt like the very air that I breathed was on fire.

Paddy said, "I need to go help."

"No, Paddy!" Caitlin shouted above the din around us. Her voice was on the edge of panic. "You stay with us."

"They need help, Caitlin." He set Tommy down by his mother and shouted, "Boys, stay with your Ma." He ran after the water pumper.

Mrs. McEneely yelled after him, "If we're not here. You'll find us on the other side of the river."

I don't know if Paddy heard her. I pushed Joseph next to his brother. I ran after my brother.

I heard Brigid scream my name, but I didn't stop.

Chapter 18

A horde of people came rushing toward us. They split apart as the firemen and water pumper drove a wedge between them. Many people were dressed in their bedtime clothes. Some carried pillow bags filled with a few snatched belongings. I felt like I was back on the Hannah. The wild looks of sheer panic were the same.

The fire grew before my eyes. The heat was unbearable. As we got closer, I saw a bucket brigade lined across the street. Men and women passed buckets of water from one to the other, but the meager buckets of thrown water did nothing to stop the fire. A cheer erupted when they saw the water pumper.

The firemen quickly set to work. They hooked up the hose and nozzle. Six firemen gathered on the each side of the pumper and began to work the long levers. One side pushed down and then the other. Water erupted from the nozzle like a geyser. The fire captain didn't even try to save the buildings engulfed in flames. He sprayed water on the buildings that hadn't caught fire.

The firemen moved like pistons in a machine. I couldn't believe how fast they pumped the levers. I knew they couldn't go on like that for long. We were too far away for the hoses to reach and suck water from the river, so the bucket brigade dumped their water into the basin of the water pump.

Red snow fell upon us. I shook my hand as a hot ember burned my knuckles. Wind was our enemy. The wind carried airborne sparks from one building to the next. I knew we were fighting a losing battle. It seemed like the entire city block was engulfed in flames.

Two horses pulling a wagon charged down the street away from the fire. The wagon was stacked with furniture a homeowner was trying to save. The furniture was burning. Sparks flew into the air as the wild-eyed horses sped by us.

One of the firemen stepped back from the pumper and collapsed. His face was covered in sooty sweat. He looked completely exhausted. My brother rushed in and took his place. Paddy grabbed the lever and fell into the firemen's rhythm of piston strokes.

I didn't know what to do. I didn't know how to help. I felt like I was just a spectator. I watched the battle to save the city unfold before me.

CHAPTER 19

Another water pumper arrived and then another. They must have come from different parts of the city. The firemen quickly went to work, but even though there were three pumpers now, they were no match for the fire. I had never seen anything like it. The fire was so intense, I felt like it could melt my skin. The fire roared. It roared like a train coming straight at me. There were loud pops and cracks as wood exploded. Buildings crumbled.

People kept running. They ran away from the fire to try and reach the safety of the river. I saw a young boy stagger out of the smoke. He was coughing. He fell to his knees. People ran around him. No one stopped.

The boy needed help. I ran to him. Smoke burned my eyes. I bent and lifted the boy over my shoulder. I staggered under his weight. I carried him back to the pumpers and fell to my knees.

The boy sat on the ground before me. His brown eyes were red, his eyebrows singed. His face was pimpled from the heat. Smoke rose from his matted, brown hair and ash-covered clothes. He coughed and coughed.

I got up and ran to the water brigade. I darted into the line and grabbed a bucket out of the hands of a startled man. I ran with the bucket back to the boy. I dumped half the water over the boy's head and shoulders.

I sank to one knee and scooped my hands into the bucket. I lifted my hands to his mouth. I shouted, "Drink."

I funneled the water between his lips. He gulped the water and then coughed. He tuned his head and vomited. When he caught his breath, I gave him more water.

The boy started shaking. He must have been about 6-years-old. He had lost his two upper baby teeth. His eyes darted every which way. I knew no nightmare could have been worse than what he was living.

He cried, "I want my ma. I want my da."

I put my hands on his shoulders to try and calm him. "It's all right. We'll find your ma and your da. What's your name?"

He stuttered, "Brady ... Brady Walsh."

"And your ma's name?"

"Mary."

"And your da?"

"Michael."

"Michael! That's my name too." I sat by him and put my arm around his shaking shoulder. "Don't cry, Brady. You're safe now. We'll find your ma and da."

The boy shook like a leaf as the flaming embers spun around us.

CHAPTER 20

Night stars disappeared. The sky lightened above the roaring flames. The captain shouted through his brass speaking trumpet for everyone to pull back. Almost the entire city block was consumed by the towering fire.

The firemen were exhausted. They quit pumping and just hung onto their levers. The water brigade line stopped. Some of the volunteer citizens sank to the ground. A few lifted their buckets to drink. One man dumped his bucket over his head.

I couldn't see what lie beyond the billowing clouds of smoke. I don't know how much of the city was destroyed.

The captain knew he had to relinquish the remains of this block to try and save another. He looked to the sky and watched the wind-borne embers. The fire would follow the embers. He pointed to the next block to the north and shouted orders to his men. Everyone started to move.

I stood. Brady scrambled up next to me. He took my hand and wouldn't let go. We walked together behind the water pumpers. Some of the firemen tried to run with the pumps, but there were too few who had the energy to join them. We trudged down the block with the fire roaring alongside us.

We walked by houses at the end of the street that were still standing. The houses were close together. The tar and shingles on some of the roofs of the houses were already on fire from the swirling red snow. People ran out into the street and beseeched the firemen to stop and save their homes, but the captain drove his men forward. We marched to the end of the street and crossed a wide avenue. We were not far from the river. I could see the steeple of St. Patrick's Church.

A fresh water pump company came running down the avenue from the north. The captain added the new water pump to the battle line he was forming. The avenue was wide, but it was bordered by wooden sidewalks on both sides.

We were now close enough that the hoses could reach the river. The captain had his pumpers soak the tinderbox houses and sidewalks behind us. A gust of wind blew red burning embers high up in the sky. The embers flew like redbirds darting above us. If the buildings behind us caught fire, I knew we would be trapped between the two fiery whirlwinds. I stood with Brady and watched the holocaust coming toward us like a fire-breathing dragon. My knees shook. I had an unbearable need to pee.

Chapter 21

People ran out of the houses that stood behind us. They carried as much as their hands could bear. A few stood on the sidewalk hypnotized by the waves of towering flames rushing toward them.

I felt like I was in a tunnel. The roar of the fiery wind was deafening. The wind blew a cloud of smoke that surrounded us like fog. There was the constant clang of bells from fire wagons and church steeples. There were screams of pain and despair. There were mournful prayers

It wasn't long before the buildings on the other side of the street in front of us were completely consumed by flames. Wind lifted flaming embers from the rooftops and carried them above the street and then above our heads. The firemen turned their hoses to the sky. They tried to shoot down the flying cinders. They looked like hunters as they sprayed streams of water at the darting redbirds. But the wind carried the embers too high up into the sunlit blue sky. I knew there was nothing we could do. The wind would carry the fire to the rooftops on the street behind us.

And then the miracle came to our rescue. The wind died. It just stopped blowing. I don't know why the wind stopped, but it did. Maybe the sun was jealous of the fire and chased the wind away. Flaming embers still rose above the inferno, but the embers stayed above the fire. There was no wind left to carry the cinders across the street.

Smoke no longer engulfed us. The smoke rose straight up into the sky above the charred buildings. It took a while for us to realize what happened, but when we did, the firemen started to cheer. Some of the grown men dropped to their knees and gave prayers of thanks. In the crowd behind us, everyone was hugging and crying.

Brady looked all around. The boy was confused. He didn't understand what just happened.

I cupped my hands on the sides of his head. I brought my face close to his. "We're safe, Brady. We're safe." His smile must have reflected my own.

Chapter 22

As only a great fire can, the fire burned itself out.

The captain stood on one of the water wagons. He gathered all his men around him and said, "We were lucky this time. If the wind would have kept blowing, this whole city would have burned to the ground and there's not a damn thing we could have done about it. We don't have the men and equipment to stop a major burn when it gets out of control." He took his hat off and wiped the soot from his face. "You can't have a city made out of wood. When there's no rain, a wooden city is just a tinderbox waiting to explode."

He pointed to the charred, smoky remains of four city blocks. "Hundreds of people lost their homes. I'm afraid to know how many lost their lives. But you men did everything that you could. I'm proud to be with you. I wish that I could send you home to your families, but I can't. We need to keep watch. The embers are still hot and the wind might come back. We need to spread out, one pumper for each block and the men to man her."

The captain climbed down from the wagon. He walked and shook hands with his firemen. He shook Paddy's hand and squeezed his shoulder. I couldn't hear what he said, but my brother nodded and smiled.

Brady still held my hand. I took him with me to join my brother.

The people and merchants of Chicago, the ones whose homes and shops were spared, brought forth food and water and passed them among the men. A saloon owner drove a horse and cart down the avenue. The firemen gave another cheer when they saw the keg of beer.

But there was sadness too. People came back, the ones who lost everything. They collapsed on the street. They sobbed in anguish as they stared at the smoking rubble and the ruins of their lives.

Some of the families, like Brady's, had been separated in the mayhem of the blaze. Parents ran down the avenue hysterically screaming names of lost loved ones.

Brady stared at the throng of people returning to their homes that were no longer there. He held tight to my hand. His eyes darted like a scared rabbit, his body twitched.

Maybe he heard his name, but I didn't. Maybe he recognized a voice. He dropped my hand and screamed, "Mama." Before I could stop him, he took off running. A woman ran out of the crowd and Brady ran right into her arms. She smothered him with her kisses and hugs. The rest of the family gathered around the mother and child.

I cried.

CHAPTER 23

We walked to Mrs. McEneely's. We were covered in grime and smelled of sweat and smoke. Our eyes were bloodshot. Paddy's teeth looked so white in his soot-streaked, bearded face.

A block away, the streets were untouched by the fire. City life went on as normal. If it wasn't for the smell of smoke that lingered in the air, you wouldn't have known there was a tremendous fire a few blocks away. People, who stared at us as we walked by, had no idea how close they came to losing their homes and shops and maybe their very lives.

My brother towered over me as he always would. Something changed in me when I ran after Paddy. I felt like I ran away from my childhood and chased the man I wanted to be. I wanted to be strong and brave like my brother. I wanted my brother to be as proud of me as I was of him.

The boys were on the porch. Thomas saw us first and came running, but Joseph quickly passed him. Paddy lifted his oldest son up in the air and spun him in a circle. Thomas grabbed hold of his da's knees and begged for his turn.

Caitlin stood on the porch with her hands wrapped around her belly. She looked like she wanted to smile, but couldn't. Brigid stood next to her sister. Her smile at me reached to her eyes.

Paddy took hold of his sons' hands and walked up on the steps. He stopped on the porch and met Caitlin's stare.

Brigid said, "Tommy and Joey, let's go inside. I'll get you some lemonade." She turned and opened the door and the boys followed her.

Paddy walked to his wife. He stopped in front of her.

Caitlin took both of his hands and turned them so that they were palm up. She ran her thumbs over his calluses. "No blisters this time." Tears flowed down her cheeks. She said in such a sad voice, "I know you're brave, Paddy, but you can't run off and leave me."

She guided Paddy's hands and rested his palms on her belly. "I can't do this by myself. You have to be here to help me."

"You knew I'd come back."

She lashed her anger at him. "How could I know? You don't know what it's like, the waiting. The not knowing if you're OK." She shook and sobbed. "I can't bear another loss."

Paddy took her in his arms. "Hush, I'm here. I'm here." He caressed her red hair and held her close as she sobbed. "I won't go anywhere without you. I promise."

I walked quietly past them into the house. I realized there was so much about life that I had yet to learn.

CHAPTER 24

Some of the Chicagoans had burns from the fire and others suffered greatly from the smoke. Mercy Hospital was overfilled. Hundreds were homeless.

Many of the homeless sought out family to stay with, but there were many like us, who had no family in Chicago. The Irish went to Father Dunne for help and the good priest brought them to Mrs. McEneely. She would turn no one away.

Many who arrived on Mrs. McEneely's doorstep were hurt and needed our rooms more than we did. So we gave them our rooms. We would spend the night in the barn with so many others who had no place to go. The plight of the sad homeless brought Ireland back to me. I knew what it was like to lose everything.

We gathered our things from the house and took them to the barn. Paddy wanted us to stay close to the door in case another fire erupted. We would sleep on hay tonight. The boys took it as another adventure. They built their small mounds of hay and then took turns jumping and falling into their new bed.

There must have been a hundred people in the barn. It reminded me of being back on the Hannah. I felt like the walls were closing in around me. I had to blink away the dizziness.

Caitlin took in our dismal surroundings and said, "It's time to move on. We're all well enough to travel. In the morning, we'll leave for Garryowen." She walked to one of her bags and dug deep to the bottom. She brought out a small purse. "Here…" She opened the purse and gave Paddy some money. "Go buy the tickets." She raised her eyes and stared. "Make sure you check the dates."

She wrinkled her nose. "You stink to high heaven. You won't be sleeping by me until you get yourself a proper bath. Stop at the barber's and get a bath and a haircut." She yanked the hair growing under Paddy's chin. "And have him shave this off. You know how it itches my face." She swung her hand in my direction. "Take your brother with you. He may not need the razor, but he needs a good soak as much as you."

Her words were gruff, but there was a smile beneath them. The fire was back in her eyes.

CHAPTER 25

I awoke early, but most of the men were already gone. The Irish may have lost their homes, but they still had their jobs. America was so different from back home. There were no jobs, no money to be made in Ireland. You could come to America with only the clothes on your back. There were jobs waiting and money to put in your pocket, money to build a house and raise a family.

In America, you could lose everything, but as long as you kept your pride, there were jobs in search of workers. You could start over. The women talked not about the homes they lost, but the new homes that they would build. They could ride the street cars and move farther out into the country. There was land waiting to be built on. They would stick together as the Irish always had in America. They would build their new Irish neighborhoods. Catholic churches and schools would follow wherever the Irish went.

Caitlin and Brigid helped Mrs. McEneely serve breakfast for her new penniless lodgers. Women from the Parish brought baskets of food. Mr. McGonigle, the baker, sent trays of fresh bread. It was so like the Irish to turn a wake into a party.

When breakfast was finished, Brigid disappeared. We went to the barn and packed our bags. Brigid came back carrying a basket of white lilies. She walked and kneeled by her belongings. She lifted the flowers from the basket and set them on the hay. She gently lifted and cuddled the small white shroud. She carefully lowered Maggie into the basket.

She arranged the lilies on top of the infant. She said a prayer and then went about gathering her things.

It felt like my journey was a journey of endless partings. It was time to say our goodbyes to Mrs. McEneely. The boys both hugged their Mrs. McEe. She smiled at the boys. I wondered if she saw her own children in the boys' faces. She gave a warm hug to Caitlin and whispered something into her ear. Caitlin hugged her back and tried to hide her tears from her children.

When it was my turn to be hugged, I remembered my ma's words. My ma told me that there are saints that walk among us.

CHAPTER 26

Paddy wanted to walk to the station. He said the walk would tucker the boys out so maybe they would sleep on the train. It was still hot and deadly dry, but there were distant clouds on the horizon that hinted at much-needed rain.

Our walk took us by St. Patrick's. The wooden scaffolds made the church seem even more imposing. St. Patrick's not only dominated the block, but the entire neighborhood. Father Dunne was talking with some workers. He pointed to the roof.

Thomas waved his pudgy fingers, but the Priest didn't notice him. The toddler took off and ran to Father Denis and, of course, Joseph ran after his brother. Paddy carried our large canvas bag on his shoulder, so it was left for me to chase after the boys.

Father Denis caught Thomas before he could crash into his knees. He smiled and lifted the child. Tommy grabbed the pectoral cross that hung from the priest's neck. The boy rubbed his grubby fingers along the silver cross. The pastor didn't seem to mind.

The rest of the family joined us. Father Denis called us each by name. I wondered how many names he knew, how many people like us the Pastor had helped through the years.

Father Denis said to Paddy, "If you have a minute, I'll take you inside." In his voice, I could hear the Pastor's pride in his church.

Paddy looked to Caitlin. She nodded her approval. Father Denis took us to a side door. We walked beneath the scaffolds.

Father Denis pulled open the door. We set our bags inside the doorway and walked into the church.

Never had I been in a church so grand. I was humbled. The boys were silent as they stared around in awe. The inside was almost finished. There were countless rows of wooden pews leading up to a beautiful altar. There was a choir loft and an arched ceiling high above our heads. There were statues of the Blessed Mother and St. Joseph. There were Stations of the Cross along the outside aisles. And, of course, there was a statue of St. Patrick. The Great Saint wore his Bishop's mitre and held his staff in one hand and a three-leaf clover in the other.

The grand church's walls were made of stone. The floors were made of marble. Sunlight beamed through beautiful stained glass windows. I thought of the countless generations of Irish who would fill the pews. I thought: This church will stand forever.

Brigid walked to the sanctuary. She kneeled on the steps going up to the altar and set the treasured basket of lilies beside her. I went and kneeled with her. The rest of our family came and joined us. Father Denis walked up the steps to the altar. He stood above us. We lowered our heads as he gave us his blessing.

I closed my eyes. I thought of the families that we left behind. How I wished my ma was here with me. She would love this church. There were wounds in my heart that would never heal.

Father Denis' prayer ended. I opened my eyes. Tommy stared at me. He left his mother and toddled over. While I kneeled, Tommy stood as tall as me. He wiped the tears from my cheeks.

CHAPTER 27

We walked out of St. Patrick's into bright sunshine. I squinted as the boys took off running. I chased, corralled, and herded them back.

Father Denis stood by Caitlin and Paddy in the shade of the scaffolds. I knew by the way my brother and sister-in-law would turn away from the priest and stare at me that I was the subject of Father Denis' conversation.

Part of me wanted Father Denis to have his way. I desperately wanted to stay. I hungered for knowledge. Chicago was like an open book bidding me to turn its pages.

Tommy darted away. I stopped him with my voice. He came back. I held my hand out and he took it.

I felt Brigid's eyes upon me. The gawky child had disappeared over the summer. Now, she was like a butterfly that spread its glorious wings. She rivaled Caitlin's beauty. I met her stare. I wished that I could look at Brigid the way she looked at me. I felt the want, the need to be held and loved in her eyes. I gazed upon her beauty. I wished my body would stir. I wished that my desire for her would grow and match her desire.

Tommy tugged at my hand like a young colt yearning to run. I checked the time. I held my pocket watch up to Paddy and swung it. He nodded and then bent and shouldered the canvas sack.

The good priest came toward us to say his goodbyes, but before he could reach us, he was intercepted by an old lady hobbling down the sidewalk with her cane. We couldn't wait. We had to go. I lifted my free hand in farewell. Father Denis nodded his goodbye.

We quickly walked the dusty, clamorous avenues of Chicago. We were pilgrims once again in search of the Promised Land, but I knew my Promised Land was already beneath my feet. I would see my family safe to Garryowen, but I knew one day, I would return to the city where I belonged.

Garryowen

CHAPTER 1

Caitlin and Paddy were befriended by Anne and her family on their crossing from Ireland. It was Anne's letter that brought us to Garryowen. We stayed with Anne's family. Anne was a small woman with a happy face and petite features. She treated us as if we were her own. Anne had six children with another on the way. One of her girls, Claire, was the same age as Brigid. It wasn't long before Brigid and Claire became best of friends. Joseph and Tommy had new brothers to tumble with.

Anne's husband, Will, took Caitlin and Paddy around and showed them the best land available. Caitlin had her heart set on a section by the creek. There was a soft rise where she wanted to build her house. She wanted a porch where she could sit and watch the sunset on her fields.

We all wore our Sunday clothes and went to the bank. Caitlin cried when Paddy signed the deed. She cried again when we had a picnic on the hill where we would build our home.

For the first time in hundreds of years, my family owned their own land.

Our neighbors came and helped raise the barn. We lived in the barn until we could build our house. Caitlin had her farm, but Paddy didn't turn out to be a farmer.

Garryowen is a small community and the Irish love to gossip. Our neighbors soon learned that my brother was skilled as a blacksmith. A local blacksmith was a man to be treasured, just like a country doctor. The closest blacksmith was in Dubuque, which was a half-day's ride away. Farmers would show up at our barn door with horses that needed to be shod and broken wagon wheel rims that needed to be fixed.

In wasn't long before Paddy bought a forge and an anvil. Word got out that there was a blacksmith in Garryowen. People came from all over the county. They'd knock on our barn door from dawn to dusk. With the constant clanging and hammering, Caitlin lost her peace and quiet. But Paddy was making money far beyond her wildest dreams.

Caitlin took over running the farm. She knew she couldn't till the fields, so she turned our farmland to pasture. We grew cows instead of grain. With the money they made from the shop and the farm, Caitlin and Paddy built a grand house that could hold a dozen children. The house was far enough away from the shop in the barn for Caitlin to enjoy her solitude.

In Ireland, the seven of us lived in a cold, smoky one-room cabin with a dirt floor and a leaky thatched roof. Now, I had my own room and a soft bed. I had glass windows, wooden floors, and oil lamps to read by. Sometimes, I wondered if my new life was just a dream.

Sunday was the day of rest. No matter how much work he had, Caitlin wouldn't let Paddy open his shop. Sunday was the day for family. We'd come home from Mass and have our Sunday meal. After our bellies were full, we'd sit on the porch and talk. Sometimes, Anne and her family would join us.

Caitlin and Paddy came from Ireland chasing a dream. Sometimes dreams do come true.

CHAPTER 2

If you want to the find the Irish, all you have to do is find a St. Patrick's Church. Garryowen's St. Patrick's was not nearly as grand as Chicago's. You could easily fit our new church inside of the St. Patrick's in the big city.

Garryowen's church reminded me of the churches we had back in Ireland. The church was built on a hill and from the steps I could see endless pastures and farmland. The church was made of stone, the floors of wood. Our new church was almost finished except for its steeple.

We wore our Sunday best for Easter Mass. Like most of the families that came to church regularly, we sat in the same pew every Sunday. Father Mazzuchelli, our pastor and founder of the parish, was a small priest with a ton of energy. He wasn't Irish. He couldn't speak a word of Gaelic, but he brought us the word of God.

The boys wore their new jackets and knickerbockers. They sat on either side of their father. They knew they must be on their best behavior if they wanted to hunt for Easter eggs after Mass.

The baby slept in Caitlin's arms. They named her Sarah after Caitlin's Ma. Caitlin was so worried when it was time for the baby to be born. No one knew if the measles would affect the infant, but Sara came out crying with all her fingers and toes and a pudgy nose. Brigid doted on her niece.

I sat on the end of the pew next to Brigid. The Irish in Garryowen were no different than the Irish back home. The married men expected a dozen children to help with their farms. There were dozens of children of all ages in the pews. There were more children than adults at Easter Mass.

Teenage boys would stare at Brigid. She was by far and away the most beautiful girl in the church. When Brigid felt their eyes lingering too long, she would take my hand and hold it in her lap to let the boys know that she was already taken.

After Mass we would visit Maggie. The cemetery was at the bottom of the hill. We'd stroll down from the church. The boys would run ahead. The cemetery was surrounded by pasture. Cows would graze on the other side of the barbed wire fence. Their ears and large brown eyes would follow us as we walked.

Each family had their own section in the cemetery. For now, Maggie was all by herself. She rested in the shade of pine trees that grew along the fence. In winter, the trees blocked the snow and cold wind. Maggie had been alone for over a year. No one knew how long it would be until one of us joined her. She had a simple marker with a Celtic cross. Brigid laid fresh lilies on the small grave. We all knelt and said a prayer. I wondered how many future generations of our family would lie next to Maggie.

I stood and brushed the dirt from my knees. I looked around at the lush, green, rolling bluffs and St. Patrick's Church on the hill above us. I knew why the Irish settled here. I felt like I was home in Ireland.

CHAPTER 3

I turned 16. I thrived in Garryowen. I hit a growth spurt. I'd still never be as tall as Paddy, but I wasn't a runt anymore. Country life was hard work and I had muscles to show for it. I had peach fuzz on my cheeks and a wisp of a mustache. I had the bane of all teenagers: pimples on my forehead.

St. Patrick's of Garryowen not only had a church but also a school. It was just a one-room school house with all the different ages mixed together. I already knew all that Mr. Stansky had to offer. I spent most of my time tutoring the younger students. I knew if I wanted to continue my education, I'd have to go elsewhere.

My days were full. After school in the evenings, I'd help Caitlin with all the paperwork needed to run a cattle farm. I'd help Paddy with the ordering and billing for the shop. It was only after the family was in bed that I'd have time for myself.

I had such a thirst for knowledge. In my bed by lamplight, I read Dr. Ryan's gift from cover to cover. When I finished his book, I ordered a book on veterinarian medicine through the mail. Caitlin now looked to me to take care of any aliments, be they human or bovine.

I loved to read. I ordered more and more books through the mail. I built shelves for my small library. I devoured Thoreau's *Walden Pond*. There would always be a special place in my heart for Walt Whitman's *Leaves of Grass*. I felt like Whitman was talking to me when he wrote:

"Not I, nor anyone else can travel that road for you.
You must travel it by yourself.
It is not far. It is within reach.
Perhaps you have been on it since you were
born, and did not know.
Perhaps it is everywhere – on water and land."

I yearned for someone to talk with about how I felt when I read his poetry. I wanted to see if other people were as moved as I was.

Caitlin and Paddy's waking hours were filled with work and family. They didn't have time for books. I tried to talk with Brigid, but reading for her was a struggle. She'd much rather bake a pie or tend to Sarah.

I knew the time had come. When the school year ends, the road I must travel would lead me away from Garryowen.

Chapter 4

We were just about to sit down at the table when Joseph and Thomas ran in from the porch.

Joseph blurted, "There's a buggy coming down our lane."

Caitlin and Paddy exchanged a look. Dinner was the only time during the day when we all sat together. Caitlin hated to have her family dinner interrupted.

"I'll see who it is," Paddy said.

Caitlin snapped at the boys, "Go wash your hands."

I wondered who would be coming at dinnertime, especially in a buggy. None of our neighbors had a buggy. Our neighbors would walk over if they wanted to visit or ride their horses. Sometimes the horses would pull a cart or a wagon. Buggies were for city folk, not for farmers. I was curious. I followed my brother to the porch.

The buggy didn't stop at the barn, but came right up to the house. I didn't recognize either the driver or passenger. The buggy stopped and a man climbed down. He was dusty and dirty from travel. He wore a large floppy hat that covered part of his face. He turned and pulled a haversack from the back of the buggy and slung it over one shoulder. He waved the driver to go. The driver flicked the reigns and turned the buggy away from our house.

The stranger walked toward us. He stopped. His eyes took in the house. He turned in a slow circle and looked at the barn and the cows in the pastures. He was a wiry man not much taller than me. He looked like he lived a hard life.

He took a step forward. He took off his hat and held it by his stomach. He eyed Paddy from head to toe and then he turned his eyes on me. He smiled through his scraggly beard. A few of his teeth were missing and the rest were yellowed.

"Hello, Michael."

Our ma always said that Danny had the voice of an angel.

CHAPTER 5

I opened my mouth to speak, but no words came out.

"You look like you've seen a ghost," Danny said. "I know the feeling. You'll get over it."

I stumbled down the steps and stood in front of my brother. "We thought you were dead."

"I'm a hard man to kill."

I expected him to vanish as I reached to touch his beard. He deflected my hand and pulled me into a rough hug. I knew it wasn't a dream. I felt his strength and smelled the sweet but yet sour stink of his body.

He pushed me away and held me at arm's length. "You look well." He squeezed my upper arms. "You've got some meat on your bones. Do you remember how we all worried about you?"

I nodded.

"Don't cry now," Danny said. "The time for tears is later when I'll tell my stories. Now, I just need to see you smile so that I know it was worth all the trouble." He turned to Paddy. "This big ox must be our brother, the one who stole the prettiest girl in Carrigillihy."

Paddy jumped down the steps. "I can't believe you're here." He bear hugged our brother. Danny disappeared into his arms.

Danny pushed away. "It's been a long day. I need a drink. Do you have any whiskey in this grand house of yours?"

"I've got a jug. Caitlin was just about to put food on the table."

"Is she well?" Danny asked in a soft voice.

"She is."

Joseph ran out onto the porch. The screen door slammed behind him. "Ma said dinner's getting cold."

Paddy grabbed his son's arm and pulled him forward. "Joseph, come meet your Uncle Danny."

Joseph shied and wouldn't leave his father's side. Danny stared at the boy. We stood in silence for a few seconds. Danny finally asked, "Joseph?"

"I named him after our da," Paddy said.

Danny reached and touched the boy's blonde locks. His lips quivered and his eyes brimmed with tears. He blinked the tears away.

"I'll take that whiskey."

I took Danny's arm and led him up the steps.

Chapter 6

Danny washed his hands in the sink, but he still smelled of the road. I wondered if that's the way I smelled during our travels from Philadelphia. He sat next to me at the table. I noticed he had a scar on his cheek above his beard.

Paddy led us in grace. Danny bowed his head, but he didn't say the prayer with us. We ate. Danny moved his food around his plate, but he ate little. He had a fondness for whiskey.

"Is the food not to your liking?" Caitlin asked.

"The food is delicious. It's my stomach. I can't eat too much, if I do …" He shrugged and then took another sip of whiskey.

Joseph stared at his uncle's hand as Danny lifted the glass.

Danny saw where Joseph stared. He set his glass down and said to the boy, "You need fast hands on a ship. A line was faster than my finger." He massaged the stump on his right hand where his index finger should be. "My finger got tangled in a line. Pop!" He pulled his left hand quickly away from the stump. "The line pulled it right off before I even knew it was gone."

Joey grimaced and asked, "Did it hurt?"

"It did." Danny flexed his hand. "Sometimes, I still think it's there even though I know it isn't." He seemed to sink into his chair as he took another sip of whiskey. He turned to Paddy. "We need to talk …" He looked at Caitlin. "But not tonight." He looked at me. "I'm just too tired. We've waited this long, another day won't matter."

"Michael," Caitlin said, "Show Danny to your room. You can sleep with the boys tonight."

Danny nodded his thanks. He used his hands to push himself up from the table. I stood with him. He wobbled a little bit. I grabbed his arm to steady him. I led him to my room. He plopped down on the bed. He fumbled with his boots. I eased him back down onto the bed and pulled his boots off. His feet smelled worse than the rest of him. He turned on his side and curled his knees up by his stomach. He started to snore.

CHAPTER 7

Danny slept the morning away. It was noon before I heard him stir. I carried a cup of coffee up to him. I found him standing in front of the shelves of my library.

"Are these your books?" he asked.

"They are. I've read them all, some more than once."

"I always knew you were the smart one in our family. Ma would be proud of you, even Da would." Danny took a book and skimmed the pages. "I can barely read a word. The only learning I had, I got from Caitlin's Ma."

"I can teach you to read."

Danny closed the book and put it back on the shelf. "I'm too old for school."

"You're not. No one's ever too old to learn."

He waved the thought away.

"Caitlin's got a bath waiting for you. She'll wash your clothes while you soak."

He scratched his beard. "I do need a bath and a shave. Will you sit with me while I soak? We can talk."

"I will."

Danny shaved off his beard, but he left a mustache that curled down around his lips. He shed his clothes. My brother was pale and scrawny. I couldn't believe that he was only two years older than me. Danny seemed as old as Paddy. He climbed naked into the tub. He sank into the steaming water that came up to his chin.

"Where have you been?" I asked.

"I was at sea. I needed time ... time to think ... time to heal, but then one day I realized I would never heal." He sank beneath the water and then reappeared. "I know all about me, tell me about you."

I told my story. The water was cold by the time I finished.

CHAPTER 8

The boys didn't know what to make of their uncle. It was like a different man joined us at the dinner table. With his beard off and his hair washed and combed back, Danny looked years younger. I forgot how blue his eyes were. He set a bottle of whiskey, which he must have brought with him in his haversack, on the table. He sat by me and winked across the table at Thomas. The boy giggled and pounded his spoon on top of his empty plate. Brigid hushed the toddler and scooped him a dollop of mashed potatoes.

As we ate, Danny pestered Paddy with one question after another. He wanted to know all about their crossing and how they came to have such a grand house. Paddy tried to talk while he ate, but his plate was still half-full when the rest of ours were empty.

Brigid cleared the plates away and Caitlin brought out an apple pie. No one could make a pie like my sister-in-law. The crust was sweet and the apples were tart. The adults drank coffee. Danny didn't use cream, but added a dash of whiskey to his cup.

The boys made quick work of their pie. Caitlin shooed them out to play while there was still light. We sat and sipped our coffee. We all stared at Danny and waited.

Danny looked at Caitlin and asked, "Have you heard from your ma and da?"

Caitlin shook her head.

"They came with us to see them off …" He motioned to me and Brigid. "After the ship sailed, they said they were going to stop and visit your brothers in Cork. That was the last time we ever saw them. Ma would go to your cottage every day to see if your parents came home. You know how fond our ma was of yours." He poured another dash of whiskey into his cup. "But they never came home. The Black Fever was upon the land. Many took sick and many died. Whole villages just disappeared." He spun his cup on his saucer. "I sorry, but that's all I know."

Caitlin dabbed her napkin on her cheeks. Brigid cried. I put my arm around her and held her close. The baby must have felt their tears. Sarah started to cry from her cradle in the parlor. Caitlin got up and left the room. She brought Sarah back with her. She sat in her chair. She slid the top of her dress down off one shoulder. She gave the baby her breast. She gently rocked back and forth and softly hummed a lullaby that her mother had hummed to her.

CHAPTER 9

"How did you find us?" Paddy asked.

Danny looked away as Caitlin took the baby from her breast and pulled her dress back up on her shoulder.

"I found a ship to Philadelphia that needed another hand. When I got to Philly, it wasn't hard to find an Irish blacksmith who lived down by the docks. I stayed with Uncle Richard and Aunty Biddy for a while to get rid of my sea legs. They're kind."

Paddy nodded.

"They knew where you lived." He smiled at Caitlin. "Your wife sent Uncle Richard and Aunt Biddy a letter with your address and news of your travels. I'm sorry to hear about Maggie." He crossed himself. "I asked them not to write about me. I wanted to surprise you. I had no idea of how far of a journey it would be. We're a long way from home."

Brigid stood and went and brought the coffee pot to the table. She refilled our cups. When she walked to Danny, he covered his cup with his hand to stop her. He poured a jigger of whiskey into his empty cup.

Danny continued his story. "We had no food and no money to buy any. There was no work to be had. After Da sent Michael off, he took a boat to England. He went to work the harvest. He promised he would return with money to get us through the winter."

Danny grew quiet. I felt like he left us and traveled back to a different time.

"We scrounged the fields during the day to find turnips and carrots and onions to put in the pot. Every night, we prayed for Da's safe return. Weeks turned into months. Da finally came home during a winter snowstorm. He was sick, but it wasn't the Black Fever. We knew it wasn't the fever because none of the rest of us got sick. He coughed and coughed. It was a wretched sound. It might have been different if we had a doctor. Ma tried her best, but there was so little she could do. Da got weaker and weaker. When he coughed, he coughed up blood. Ma held his hand as he died."

Danny lifted and swirled the whiskey in his cup. "There was no one to help us. All our neighbors were gone. I was only 10. I didn't know how to make a casket. I buried Da in the bloody sheet that he died on. I buried him next to his da on the hill."

Danny drained his cup. "We survived the winter on the money Da brought back from England."

I always thought the hardest thing was not knowing what happened to my da, but I was wrong.

CHAPTER 10

The boys chased fireflies in the twilight. Joseph had the knack of it. He'd catch and gently hold a firefly in his hand. He'd bring his treasure up to us on the porch. He'd slowly open his little hand. He'd blow on the firefly and its wings would take flight. He'd laugh and then run to catch another.

Tommy ran around the yard. He hadn't figured out the game. He tried to catch fireflies with an open hand. All he did was shoo them away, but he enjoyed the chase.

Caitlin sat on her rocking chair on the porch. Sarah slept in her arms. Brigid sat beside her sister. They both watched the joyful boys and the glorious sunset behind them. It was a beautiful spring night. The type of night that made you feel good.

Danny sat on the porch steps. I sat on one side of him and Paddy the other. It was so strange for us all to be together after so long apart.

Danny said, "The money Da brought home from England didn't last through the winter. When we couldn't pay the rent, Coghlan ..." It was like he spit the name "... came with the Sheriff and Lord Townsend's notice to quit. Mary and I had to drag Ma out of the cottage or Coghlan's men would have tumbled our home around her. Ma collapsed in the road and wailed. She shook her rosary at heaven and begged for God's help."

Danny reached into his pocket and took out a pouch of tobacco. He rolled a cigarette and offered it to Paddy. My older brother shook his head. Danny struck a match and lit his cigarette. He blew a cloud of pungent smoke.

"The sheriff took us to the workhouse. There were hundreds of starving Irish, who looked like walking skeletons, gathered outside the gates. The English had closed the soup kitchens and now the only place to get soup was in the workhouse. But you needed papers to get through the gate. Most of the Irish had no papers. The sheriff had our eviction notice so they had to let us in. Black Fever was rampant in the workhouse. Every day a cart would come and take the dead away. The matron separated the men from the women. They would go to separate quarters. They took children from their mothers. Ma held me fierce. She wouldn't let go. They tore me away from her and put me with the other boys. That was the last time I saw our ma."

Tommy finally caught a firefly. He ran to us and opened his hand. The lightning bug crawled long his palm. Danny placed his finger next to the firefly. The bug crawled up on his finger. Danny lifted his hand and gently blew. The lighting bug took flight. It blinked as it rose up into the night sky.

Chapter 11

The boys gave their hugs and kisses. Brigid took them inside to get them settled for the night.

Danny stood and stretched. He said, "Can we walk for a while."

The moon was up. Paddy led us down the lane that went out to the road. We walked three abreast.

"I had a friend," Danny said, "who snuck me to the workhouse's chapel. Mary and Joanna waited in the chapel after Mass to meet with me. I didn't recognize them at first. They were dressed in such finery. They were among the few girls chosen to be sent from the workhouse to Australia. They wanted single girls of childbearing age to make the long voyage. Our sisters were given fine clothes and their passage was paid. They had new shoes and bonnets. Mary and Joanna were excited to leave, excited with the promise of a new life. It didn't matter if they had to work the rest of their lives to pay back what they owed for their crossing. They knew any life had to be better than life in the workhouse."

"So they're alive," Paddy said.

"I know they left. I don't know what became of them." Danny looked up at the stars. "I hope they are." He hugged his arms to his chest as if he was suddenly cold. "They told me that Ma had died. Ma slept between our two sisters. One morning, she just never woke up. I think part of Ma died when Da died, part of her died when they tumbled her cottage. Ma didn't have much life left when she entered the workhouse."

We got to the end of our lane. We turned and walked back to the house. Fireflies glowed and crickets chirped.

"There was no reason for me to stay at the workhouse. There was no one to stay for. I had to find our ma's grave before I could leave. There were too many dead for coffins and markers. The English dug a pit in the ground and threw the dead in the pit. I said a prayer at the edge of the pit where Ma laid with thousands of others who died during the time of our holocaust."

Danny shoved his hands in his pockets. He shuffled his feet along the dirt lane.

My soft voice broke as I said, "At least Ma wasn't alone when she died." I went to Danny and hugged him. "I never should have taken your place. I had no idea how you have suffered. Will you ever forgive me?"

"There's nothing to forgive. I'm your big brother. It was my job to protect you, to keep you safe."

I cried for my ma. I held onto Danny to keep from falling. I cried for my da. I cried for my sisters. I cried for all the Irish who suffered and died. I cried for Danny.

I felt Paddy's strong arms circle around us. We stood as brothers beneath the stars on our farm in Garryowen. We cried for all that we had lost.

Chapter 12

Paddy wanted to have a party, a grand party to celebrate Danny's coming to Garryowen. The party would be at our house on a Sunday after Mass. But we needed a day when the weather would be obliging.

We waited for the spring rains to end. Finally, on a sunny day on the cusp of summer, we had our party.

Caitlin was beside herself with worry. It might be Danny's party, but it was her house where people would gather. She wanted everything to be perfect. Caitlin and Brigid spent weeks scrubbing the floors and washing the windows. Our house never looked grander.

The neighbors all knew the way to our doorstep. At one time or another, they had all stopped at Paddy's shop. Anne and her family were the first to arrive. Anne quickly took charge and assigned us all a task. We carried our table out on the lawn. Anne and a few others brought their tables and chairs from their homes in their wagons. We made a line of tables that stretched across the front of the house.

One after another, families arrived. Our lane was full of parked wagons. Each neighbor came with a dish to be shared. More than a few men brought their jugs. Our yard was soon full with a kaleidoscope of colors. Everyone still wore their Sunday best. Everywhere I looked, there were children of all ages laughing and darting about.

Some of the men brought their fiddles, flutes, and tin whistles. The musicians gathered on our porch. They played their glorious music. Our neighbors sat at the tables and tapped their feet as they ate.

I thought of Uncle Seamus. No one could play the fiddle like him. I so wished he was with us.

Teenagers gathered together at the tables farthest away from the music and away from the prying eyes of their parents. I knew many of them from school. I walked over to join them. The girls were coy. The boys were loud and boisterous.

A youth sat by himself at the end of the table. I had never seen him before. He was one of our blue-eyed Irish who had black hair. He was striking. He had sharp cheekbones and a strong chin. His face and arms were tanned by the sun. He had the look of a noble prince of old. I felt like the boy came to life from one of my dreams. He stared across the yard at a girl serving punch to the children. He couldn't take his eyes off Brigid. I couldn't take my eyes off him.

CHAPTER 13

I wanted to be near him, to hear his voice, to make sure that he was real. I walked and pulled out a chair. I sat at the table across from the boy. He looked at me. He seemed as if he was trying to figure out who I was. I wanted to touch him.

I held out my hand. "I'm Michael."

He put his fork down and extended his hand. "I'm Cillian."

I said, "We've never met."

"We haven't. I just arrived last week."

The boy seemed to be about my age. He didn't have the look nor the voice of a boy not long from Ireland.

I asked with surprise in my voice, "From Ireland?"

He laughed. "No, from Ohio. We sold our farm there and bought one here that's twice the size." He pointed off to the west. "It's a good piece of land on the other side of the river. My dad says if we have a good harvest, we'll buy more land. My dad aims to be rich and he might be right. The land's fertile here. We now can grow twice the corn we grew in Ohio."

He stared at me. I felt myself blush.

"What about you? Where's your farm?"

"It's right beneath our feet."

He laughed. He must have thought I was joking.

"Actually it's my brother's land. Paddy's the blacksmith and this is his farm. This party's for my brother, Danny, who finally found his way here from Ireland."

"I've heard of the local blacksmith. They say he does good work."

"He does."

"I'll tell my dad. We have a couple of mares that need to be shod."

Cillian looked past me to the tables behind us. He asked, "Do you know the girl over there. The one serving punch?"

I didn't have to turn to look where he pointed. "I do. She lives her too. She's my sister-in-law. Her name is Brigid."

Cillian's mouth made an O of surprise. "Can you introduce me?" He lowered his eyes. "I think she's beautiful and I want to meet her." He scrunched his shoulders and sank down in his chair. "But I just sit here and stare. I'm too shy to walk over and introduce myself."

I stared at Cillian and then I turned and looked at Brigid. Her eyes sparkled and she laughed as she handed a young girl a cup of punch. I turned back to Cillian. I could get lost in his eyes, but I knew he would never look at me the way he looked at Brigid. He stared at me expectantly.

I stood up. "Come on. I'll take you to meet her."

Cillian got up so fast that he knocked his chair over. He followed in my footsteps as we walked to the girl serving punch.

"Brigid, you have a new admirer," I said.

It was the boy's turn to blush. The rose in his cheeks only made him look more beautiful.

"His name's Cillian. He's a new neighbor. He wanted to meet you."

Brigid's eyes took in the boy. She smiled a demure smile, but it didn't stop at her lips – the smile went to her eyes. She lifted a cup of punch and offered it to the boy.

Cillian's hand shook as he took the cup. Punch splashed over his fingers, but I don't think he noticed.

I don't think either one of them minded as I turned and walked away.

CHAPTER 14

I went in search of my brother. He wasn't at any of the tables where the youths had gathered. Maybe he felt he didn't belong. Danny was only two years older than me, but sometimes, I felt he was a generation away.

I asked if anyone had seen him, but no one had. I found Joseph and Thomas playing with their friends. I asked Joseph if he had seen his uncle. He pointed to the barn. I could see Danny from where I stood in the yard. He was up in the loft. The loft door was open. He sat by himself. His feet dangled over the edge

I walked to the barn and went inside. I climbed the ladder. I went and sat by my brother. From the loft, we could see the yard below. We could see the tables brimming with food and our Irish neighbors talking, eating, and laughing. The wind carried music from the porch.

Danny offered me his whiskey bottle. I shook my head. He took a gulp.

"It's too much," he moaned.

It took me a second to understand his words. He had spoken in Gaelic. It was a long time since I heard my native tongue.

He pointed the bottle at the tables. "They don't know what it was like." He set the bottle between us. "The few who do, they don't want to remember. But I will never forget."

He turned to me. I couldn't look away. His eyes were bloodshot. His pupils were huge. His breath stank of whiskey.

"Do you see the ghosts among them, Michael? The dead we left behind, the ones who died so that we could live. I know Paddy doesn't see them because he wasn't there, but you were there, Michael. You walked among the dead." He pointed to the Irish in our yard. "Do you see the ghosts out there? They're walking among the living. They want their place at the table."

My brother scared me. I didn't know if it was the whiskey or if Danny was losing his mind.

I touched his shoulder. "Let's go get you something to eat, Danny."

He pushed my hand away. "Do you remember the winter? The snow and how cold it was. There was nothing left to eat. I went outside to search for food, but there was nothing to find. My fingers bled as I tore bark from the trees. I'd carried the bark home. Ma boiled the bark in her pot and called the brown water soup. That was our dinner." He jabbed his fist at the tables in the yard. "What we would have given to sit at one of those tables."

His hand fell to his lap. He grew quiet as he stared at the tables.

"Sometimes, it's not good to be alone, Danny. You need to come with me."

I stood and moved behind my brother. I bent and slid my hands under his armpits and pulled him to his feet. He wobbled and then steadied.

"Wait." He bent and picked up his bottle.

I took his arm and led him to the ladder.

CHAPTER 15

It was a night I'll never forget, a night that magically took me back to the Ireland of my childhood. The dinner was finished and the jigs and reels began. Our neighbors left their tables and gathered in the open space in front of the porch. The wee ones abandoned their games. They ran to join us.

Music is the soul of the Irish. I can't hear a lively fiddle without wanting to dance.

It was a night full of surprises. The music must have possessed Caitlin. She took Paddy's hand and pulled him before the musicians. She started to dance and Paddy followed. The sight of them took me back to their wedding when they were only 16. They danced with an abandon that only the young possess. Now, as they danced, Caitlin tried to recapture that youth and she did. They danced and spun as one. Caitlin glowed. Her fiery red hair flew atop her shoulders. Joey and Tommy stood spellbound as they stared at their parents. Faster and faster the music played and faster and faster Caitlin and Paddy danced.

The reel ended. Caitlin stopped. She fell into her husband's embrace. Joey and Tommy ran and hugged their parents. Joey hugged their waists and Tommy hugged their knees. Our neighbors clapped and cheered.

Brigid stood across the yard. She stared at her sister with such a look of yearning. Cillian stood beside her.

No one wanted the party to end. The music went on and on. Our yard was full of Irish dancers. When the adults grew tired, their children took their places. The wee ones looked like Irish fairies spinning in the twilight. Their parents sat at the tables and clapped their hands to the music.

When the musicians could play no more, they took a break. They wet their whistles from their jugs and lit their corn pipes.

It was a night for new friends to be made and old ones to be reacquainted. It was a night for stories to be shared and cakes and pies to be devoured.

I walked among our neighbors. I didn't see the ghosts of our past as Danny did. I saw the children of our future.

CHAPTER 16

I sat with Danny at the table. He ate little, but drank more. The party whirled around him, but he seemed trapped in the past. Our neighbors tended to avoid him. They could see the morose cloud that hovered over my brother. Even Thomas and Joseph avoided their uncle.

The musicians snuffed out their smoking pipes. They made their way back to the porch. They picked up their instruments. Paddy went and talked with them and then came and sat with us.

The fiddler moved to the front of the porch and stood by the steps. I knew from the first few notes what song he would play. He played the first stanza. It was such a melancholy melody. The music stirred my heart and brought back so many memories. Our neighbors grew quiet. Joseph crawled up on his da's lap and Tommy crawled up on mine.

The fiddler stopped and then started again from the beginning. Danny stood. He stood straight and tall. He sang the words with a strong, haunting voice as the fiddler played:

> "The Minstrel-Boy to the war is gone
> In the ranks of death you'll find him;
> His father's sword he has girded on,
> And his wild harp slung behind him.
> 'Land of song!' said the warrior-bard,
> Tho' all the world betrays thee,
> One sword, at least, thy rights shall guard,
> One faithful harp shall praise thee!"

I was back in our cottage. Danny stood by the hearth as Uncle Seamus fiddled beside him. Danny sang with the voice of an angel. He sang our da's favorite song. The song that always made our da cry.

The Minstrel fell!—but the foeman's chain
Could not bring that proud soul under;
The harp he lov'd ne'er spoke again,
For he tore its chords asunder;
And said, "No chains shall sully thee,
Thou soul of love and bravery!
Thy songs were made for the pure and free,
They shall never sound in slavery."

The music faded into the still night air. Not a word was spoken. More than one of our neighbors wiped tears from their eyes.

Danny raised his glass and toasted the fiddler. He snatched his bottle. He walked away from the table. He walked in the shadows of the sunset back to the barn.

CHAPTER 17

The party had tuckered out both the young and the old. Parents carried the wee ones in their arms and on their shoulders. Some of the children were already asleep before their parents gently laid them in the back of their wagons. Young lovers, who had snuck off to the pastures, now snuck back to join their families. The musicians played soft music. A few dancers still lingered entwined in the moonlight and soft glow of lanterns.

Men loaded up their wagons with the tables and chairs that they had brought. Paddy had started a fire to burn the refuse of the party. A few of the Irish didn't want the night to end. They gathered around the flames to escape the chilly early summer night air. A jug was passed. I thought, what we needed was a storyteller, but we left our storytellers behind in Ireland.

I stood beside the roaring flames. Brigid and Cillian came out of the darkness and stood on the other side of the fire. Cillian's hand danced and hovered like a butterfly next to Brigid, but he didn't touch her. Cillian said something to make Brigid laugh. The boy had a ready smile. He seemed like a lad who had lived a happy life. I wondered if he would make Brigid a happy wife and give her her own children to love. I snuck away and let them be.

I went to the barn. I lit a lantern and carried it up the ladder to the loft. I could hear Danny's loud, gulping snores before I saw him. My brother had passed out. The whiskey bottle must have rolled off his chest. The uncorked bottle rested beside him. The hay was damp with spilled whiskey.

I set the lantern down. I pulled Danny away from the edge of the loft. He stirred, but didn't awaken. I closed and bolted the loft's door. I rolled him on his side and pushed a bale of hay behind him. If he got sick in the night, I hoped at least he wouldn't get sick all over himself.

I lifted the lantern and shined the light on my brother. I tried to see the little boy curled inside the drunken man on the floor. I tried to find the boy whose place I took on the crossing. Where did that boy go and how could I get him back? Danny was only 18. He had his whole life ahead of him.

I realized there was nothing more that I could do, so I took the lantern and left my brother to his stupor.

Chapter 18

The sun rose on Monday morning. I awoke to the roosters' cock-a-doodle-doos and the cows' mooing. There were chores that needed to be done. I wondered if everyone was as tired as me. I didn't want to, but I climbed out of my warm bed.

Brigid seemed lost in thought as she served me breakfast. If our eyes met, she would look away. I knew I had to talk with her, but first I had to find the right words to say.

I went to the barn to check on Danny. I didn't have to climb the ladder. I could hear his loud snores coming from the loft above me. I let him be and set about my chores.

Danny joined us for dinner. I could tell by Joseph's face that the young boy was still trying to figure out who was this strange man that sat at his table.

Danny was ghastly pale. There was hay stuck in his uncombed hair. His clothes reeked of stale whiskey. His fork shook as if lifted it to his mouth. He set the fork down and hid his shaking hands in his lap under the table.

Danny pushed his hands against his stomach and rocked in his chair. He looked at Paddy and asked, "Can I see the watch?"

Paddy's face showed surprise – or was it dread? He turned to Caitlin. A look passed between them that conveyed so much more than words. Caitlin slowly nodded.

"It's gone," Paddy said.

Danny stopped rocking. He stared at Paddy and waited.

"Uncle Seamus warned us about the runners," Paddy said. "But I didn't know the runners would be Irish. They cheated us out of the money we had left to get to Philadelphia." Paddy curled his hand around his coffee mug. "It was winter. We had no money. We had no food. We knew no one in New York. We had no place to shelter."

Paddy looked at his wife. Caitlin nodded for him to go on.

"There were no jobs. I knew we wouldn't make it through the winter. We had to get out of New York. We had to get to Uncle Richard in Philly."

Paddy's face hardened. He stared at Danny. He said in a voice that would bear no argument, "I had no choice. I sold the watch and used the money to buy two train tickets to Philadelphia."

Danny shook his finger at Paddy. "That watch was the only tie we had to our past. Our great-grandfather got that watch from the French when they came to help us fight against the English." He pounded his fist on the table. "He died for that watch. You had no right to sell it. That watch was the only thing of value our family has ever had."

I closed my hand over my brother's fist. "You're wrong, Danny. The only thing of value that we have ever had is sitting at this table. Our lives, Danny, that's the only thing of value that we have."

Danny snatched his hand away from mine. He angrily shoved his chair back. He rose and stormed out of the kitchen.

Joey and then Tommy started to cry.

CHAPTER 19

I knew it was useless to go search for Danny. He'd come home when he was ready. I sat on the porch steps with Paddy. My brother was quiet. He brooded and stared out into the darkness.

Paddy cracked the knuckles of one hand and then the other. "I had no choice."

"You had a choice, Paddy," I said. "You made the right choice."

The voice came from the darkness, "You did, Paddy."

Danny walked out of the dark. He seemed to leave his anger behind as he walked into the light from the window. "I was wrong to say what I did. Sometimes my temper gets the best of me. Da sent you here to survive. You did what you had to in order to survive."

Danny climbed the steps and sat between us. He put his hand on Paddy's shoulder. "Da would be proud of you. Do you remember what he said, he told you to go first and make a home for the rest of us."

Paddy nodded. "I do."

"You did it Paddy. You survived." Danny swept his hand out to the pasture. "And look at what you built."

Paddy faced his brother. "There's a place for you here, Danny. Or if you'd rather, I'll give you money to buy your own farm."

Danny shook his head. "I can't stay. I only came here to say my goodbyes."

I didn't know what my brother was talking about. "But where will you go?" I asked.

"I'll go home. I never should have left. I swore on our ma's grave that she would be avenged. I swore on da's grave and the graves of our ancestors that they would be avenged. The English ..." Danny hacked and spat on the ground. "The English ruled us with an iron fist for 700 years. They kept us dirt poor and ignorant. When we rebelled, they hung us. When the famine came, they took our grain and left us to starve. They evicted us from our farms and sent us to the workhouse. Over a million of us have died during the time of the Great Hunger. Another million of us have had to flee the land of our birth and come to America."

"There's life for us here," Paddy said. "Life beyond the wildest dreams we ever had in Ireland."

"But it's not our home. Our home is Ireland."

"You're wrong, Danny. We're Irish. It doesn't matter where our feet are, our blood is Irish. No one can take that away from us. My children and their children will be Irish no matter where they live."

"But what of the ones we left behind," Danny implored. "What is to become of them?"

"It's not our fight. We left that fight behind. Our life is here."

"It may not be your fight," Danny said. His always simmering anger was set to boil. "But it's mine. There are men like me who will never forget nor forgive what the English did to us. There are men like me who will fight."

"They'll kill you. They'll hang you just like just like they hung our great-grandfather."

Danny said forlornly, "You can't kill a man who's already dead."

"Don't go, Danny," I pleaded. "Stay with us."

"The Fenians have guns. I know ships and how to smuggle guns on them to Ireland. If it's one thing that I learned, we need guns to beat the English."

"Don't do it," Paddy said in the voice of an older brother who thought he still had say over his younger sibling. "Stay here."

Danny sadly shook his head. "Your life is here, not mine." He stood and stared at Paddy. "Take care of your children. Keep them close. I'll be leaving in the morning."

He came and put his hands on my shoulders. He stared at me as if he was trying to etch my face into his mind. "I made the right choice." He squeezed my shoulders. "I would do it again." He leaned and kissed my forehead just like our ma used to kiss us goodnight. He walked up the steps and then into the house.

That was the last time I ever saw my brother. Danny wasn't one for goodbyes. He left before the sun rose in the morning.

CHAPTER 20

The house changed when Danny left. It wasn't so much that it changed, it just went back to the way things used to be before Danny came. I tried to help out as much as I could during the long summer days. I knew I'd leave in the fall.

I corresponded with both Father Dunne and Dr. Ryan. Between the two of them they secured me a spot in the medical class that would start at Mercy Hospital in September. I had my brother's blessing and, more importantly, financial backing. I wouldn't be a starving student in Chicago. Caitlin surprised me when she pushed me to go and follow my dreams. But I think she knew that I was different and that I wasn't meant to be a farmer. Or maybe she just fell in love with the idea of being able to tell her neighbors that she had a doctor in her family.

Sundays was always the day of rest. The days grew hot. After Mass, we'd picnic down by the river. The boys found a new pastime. They discovered that there were fish in our stream. They'd wade barefoot into the shallow water until it was up to their knees. They tried to catch fish with their bare hands. They never caught any, but that didn't stop them from trying.

Brigid sat on the bank and kept an eye on the boys. Across the river there were fields of golden sunflowers. Butterflies danced above the swaying flowers.

We had been avoiding each other since the night of the party. I knew she knew of my leaving, but we had yet to talk. I couldn't leave with the words unsaid.

I summoned my courage and sat next to Brigid.

"Remember when you were little and you would chase butterflies," I asked.

Brigid seemed surprised by the question. She said, "You'd chase them with me."

"I would."

We fell silent. We watched the boys and the beautiful dancing butterflies behind and above them. As children it was so easy for us to talk and now it seemed so hard.

I said softly, "You know I love you."

She wouldn't look at me. I wished that I could see her blue eyes beneath her bonnet, but she just stared at the boys. She wouldn't make it easy.

I took a breath and sighed, "You need to find another. I'm not the man you need me to be. I can't be something that I'm not. Wishing it won't change anything."

I pushed up from the ground and stood above her.

"I will always love you, Brigid."

I turned and walked away.

CHAPTER 21

I dreaded the day of my leaving, but I so wanted to go. I spent as much time as I could with the boys. They were growing so fast.

Joseph watched as I packed my haversack. Tommy sat on the bed. He rolled a ball of my socks above my blanket.

"But you'll come back," Joseph cried.

"Of course I will." I tried to make my voice sound happy. "I'll be back for Christmas. I'll bring you and Tommy a gift. You need to tell your ma what you want and have her write it down in a letter and send it to me."

Joseph pouted and whined, "But why do you have to go?"

"Because I want to be doctor and if I'm going to a doctor I have to go away to school. It takes a long time and a lot of studying to become a doctor."

"Don't go," Joseph said.

The boy could be as stubborn as his mother. "Remember when we all had the measles and Dr. Ryan helped us."

Joseph nodded.

"That's what I want to do. I want to be a doctor and help people. Remember when Tommy had his earaches."

I picked the little one up off the blanket. I puckered my lips and blew raspberries on his neck. Tommy laughed and squirmed in my arms. I blew some more. The wee one laughed and tried to push me away.

"The doctor made his ear all better. That's what I want to do. I want to make people better. That's why I have to go away to school."

I set Tommy on the floor. I knelt before him. I motioned Joseph to come join us. I curled one palm on Tommy's hair and the other on Joseph's.

I looked at Joseph and said, "You're the older brother. Your job is to take of your little brother. Can you do that?"

Joseph nodded.

I turned to Tommy. "And Tommy, your job is to listen to Joseph and to help your brother. Can you do that?"

Tommy nodded.

"You'll always be brothers." I said softly, yet solemnly, "And you'll always love each other."

I thought of Danny. I pulled the boys to me and hugged them. I didn't want them to see me cry.

Chapter 22

My young life was a life of partings and new beginnings.

Paddy had the wagon ready. He would take me to Dubuque. From there I would take a barge across the river and then the train to Chicago.

We said our goodbyes on the porch. I looked out at the farm. Anne was right, Garryowen was so like Ireland. The air was fresh and pure. The rolling hills were lush and green.

Caitlin packed me a basket for my travels. Leaving her was like leaving my mother again. When she hugged me, I could feel the bump of her stomach and the life growing inside her.

Brigid lingered by the doorway. I nodded my goodbye. She ran to me and hugged me so fiercely that I couldn't breathe.

She said, "I love you, Michael."

I gently unwound her arms. "I have to go."

"I know." Her hand softly cupped my face. "If only we could have stayed children."

I took her hand. "If only …" I kissed her fingers.

Brigid turned and ran into the house.

I climbed up on the wagon. Paddy flicked the reigns and the horses lumbered down the lane that led from one life to another.

The boys ran out of the house and down the porch steps. They shouted, "Michael, Michael." They waved their arms and ran after the wagon. Tommy stumbled and fell. He started to cry.

Joseph stopped. He ran back to help his brother.

Author's Note

The Feeneys, on my mother's side of my Irish ancestry, fled County Roscommon, Ireland during the 1840s to escape the potato famine. Patrick and his wife, Catherine, had seven children. Both parents died on a famine ship during the voyage to America and joined over one million Irish who perished during the time of the Great Hunger. One of their sons, my great-great-grandfather Thomas Feeney, survived the crossing. He worked his way across America until he settled in Garryowen, Iowa where he farmed the fertile land and helped to build St. Patrick's Church.

On my father's side of my Irish family, Richard O'Leary left County Cork, Ireland in the 1880s as part of the chain of the many millions of Irish who emigrated to a new life in America. There were over 8 million people in Ireland before the start of the potato famine. By the time Ireland achieved independence in 1921, the population of Ireland was less than 4 million people.

The Minstrel Boy was written by Thomas Moore. It is widely believed that Moore composed the song in remembrance of his friends who were killed in the Irish Rebellion of 1798.

I am indebted to Sister Mary Angela Feeney, P.B.V.M. and Patrick L. Colman who helped inspire this story. They gathered the history of my ancestors in their book *At Grandpa's Knee*.

My grandmother, Irma Cannon, lived to be almost 100 years old. Her stories of my Irish heritage will always live within me.

Many thanks go to Dennis Bova for his years of friendship and editorial assistance.

I live in the shelter of my family.

www.ingramcontent.com/pod-product-compliance
Lightning Source LLC
Chambersburg PA
CBHW031133210626
46816CB00014B/692